Untraveled

Treasure Hunter Security #5

D1596732

Anna Hackett

Untraveled

Published by Anna Hackett
Copyright 2017 by Anna Hackett
Cover by Melody Simmons of eBookindiecovers
Edits by Tanya Saari

ISBN (eBook): 978-1-925539-29-5
ISBN (paperback): 978-1-925539-30-1

What readers are saying about
Anna's Romances

Unexplored – Romance Writers of Australia Ruby Finalist 2017

At Star's End – One of Library Journal's Best E-Original Romances for 2014

Return to Dark Earth – One of Library Journal's Best E-Original Books for 2015 and two-time SFR Galaxy Awards winner

The Phoenix Adventures – SFR Galaxy Award Winner for Most Fun New Series and "Why Isn't This a Movie?" Series

Beneath a Trojan Moon – SFR Galaxy Award Winner and RWAus Ella Award Winner

Hell Squad – Amazon Bestselling Science Fiction Romance Series and SFR Galaxy Award for best Post-Apocalypse for Readers who don't like Post-Apocalypse

The Anomaly Series – #1 Amazon Action Adventure Romance Bestseller

Chapter One

She slammed into the interrogation room.

Special Agent Elin Alexander strode across the small space, ignoring the nervous look from the man handcuffed to the desk. The heels of her boots clicked on the floor, and she took her time setting her files and coffee down. Then she put her hands on her hips, which pulled the edges of her jacket apart.

The man's gaze jumped to the Glock 23 holstered on her right hip. He swallowed, sweat beading on his forehead.

"Mr. Dennison, you aren't having a very good day, are you?"

The man shifted in his seat. "I don't know anything."

"Right." Elin sat down.

She eyed the man. Mark Dennison was extremely low-level at the black-market antiquities syndicate, Silk Road. But with his slim build, greasy brown hair, and muddy brown eyes, he was very good at being ignored. She knew he'd been around at some of the planning meetings for the group's latest expedition to plunder an ancient site.

"I know about the mission to the Kalahari. I want to know everything you know about it."

He shook his head. "They'll kill me." His gaze met hers for a second before darting away. "And when Claude finds out you're an FBI mole, he'll leave you full of bullet holes and bleeding in a dirty alley somewhere."

Elin leaned back in her chair. Claude Renard, leader of the local Silk Road cell she'd infiltrated, didn't worry her.

What worried her was that this damn group was once again planning to kill and steal, to take pieces of history and desecrate them. Sell them for profit, and not give one thought to the lives they'd ruin in the process.

They didn't care about little girls who were left fatherless, and mothers whose careers were destroyed.

Elin banged a fist on the table and Dennison jumped. "You tell me what you've heard. I know the plan is to find a lost city in the Kalahari. I want to know what else they're after."

Because she knew Claude was after more than the tumbled ruins of a long-dead city. He was after something. Something valuable.

Dennison's throat bobbed as he swallowed. "They'll kill me."

She pushed her chair back and circled the table. The man stiffened, staring at the surface of the desk.

Elin stalked closer, resting her hands on the back of the man's chair, and lowered her voice. "If you tell me nothing, I'll let you go…"

He blinked, his brow creasing. "What?"

She leaned closer, her mouth close to his ear, and when the scent of unwashed body hit her, she hid her grimace. "And I will ensure everyone knows that you were in FBI custody, and that you sang like the prettiest little songbird."

"No."

"Yes." She moved back to her chair. "But, you tell me everything you've heard, guessed, or been told, then I'll sneak you out of here and ensure you do your time at a prison on the other side of the country."

He lifted his cuffed hands to his mouth, nibbling on a ragged nail. "Claude's after a treasure. Something really, really valuable."

"What?"

"I don't know! I swear. He's been careful with what he's said."

"What else?"

"One of the top dogs is sponsoring the trip. Dealing directly with Claude."

Excitement shot through Elin, and she leaned forward. "One of the top leaders of Silk Road?"

Dennison nodded. "Claude's jazzed about it. Said that when he nails this mission and delivers the treasure, he'll finally break into the inner circle."

This could be it. Elin's thoughts whirled. A chance to crack the mysterious and dangerous group open…and finally bring them down. She looked up at the mirrored window.

She pushed a notepad and pen across the table.

ANNA HACKETT

"Write it all down. Everything."

When she stepped out of the room, her boss was waiting for her.

"Nice work," Special Agent Alastair Burke said.

"Thanks." Elin smiled with grim satisfaction. "This could be it, Alastair."

"We could finally find out who the hell is behind Silk Road." He stared through the window at Dennison. "If we can trust this guy."

Burke was tall, dark, and slightly too intense for handsome. With brown hair cut short, green eyes, and a faint shadow of stubble on his hard jaw, he was the poster child for dedicated, dangerous FBI agent. Elin respected the hell out of him, and never regretted her decision to join the Art Crime Team under his leadership.

If there was anyone more determined to bring down Silk Road than her, it was Alastair Burke. Sometimes, she wondered what drove him.

"You ready for the mission to Africa?" he asked.

She nodded. "I'm ready. I'll be traveling tomorrow to Cape Town to meet Claude and the others." She smiled. "Sure you won't spring for Business Class? It's a long flight."

A slight smile. "Suck it up, Alexander."

She glanced at her watch. "One last thing I have to do is meet the Treasure Hunter Security agent you're sending in with me."

"Hale Carter," Alastair said with a nod. "He's solid. Former Navy SEAL with good skills."

"You're sure it's necessary to bring THS in?" She knew the security company had skilled people and

4

specialized in providing security for archeological digs and expeditions, but this was *her* mission.

"You're FBI, Elin. You'll be operating in South Africa and Namibia only with the cooperation of the local agencies. I can't take a large team into foreign nations without stepping on a hell of a lot of toes. But, I do want you to have backup I can trust."

"I'm going to stop Silk Road. And if Dennison is right, we'll bring down one of the heads of the snake at the same time."

Alastair nodded. "You do this, Elin, and that promotion to the Interpol task force that you've been wanting is all yours."

She barely controlled her reaction. For the last two years, that promotion was the thing she'd been living and breathing for. It would give her greater reach to take down Silk Road and other organizations like it. "You can count on me."

Alastair gripped her shoulder and squeezed. It wasn't common for him. He wasn't a toucher. "You've never let me down."

She nodded. "I need to get to this meeting with Carter."

"Elin?" His green eyes flashed. "Stay safe."

She nodded again. "Will do."

She and Alastair parted ways, and Elin stopped by her borrowed office to grab her things. The Art Crime Team had permanent offices in DC, but they were used to flying all around the country and borrowing space in the local FBI offices. The team in Denver was getting pretty used to her and Burke.

The slim folder on her desk caught her eye and she flicked it open, even though she'd memorized all the information in there.

A picture of Hale Carter rested on top.

It was a formal military shot. He was in his Navy dress whites, smiling for the camera. The man had a hell of a smile. Dark skin she knew came from his mother, handsome face inherited from his father, and intelligence in his gorgeous velvet-brown eyes.

She'd been through his file. She always did her research before a mission. Hale Carter had been a very good Navy SEAL, but when his final mission had gone bad, and his team had been killed, Carter had been the only survivor. He'd spent a month in a military hospital recovering, and after they slapped a medal on him for bravery, he'd left the Navy. She wondered what demons that smile was hiding.

He'd ended up with the Ward family—former SEALs Declan and Callum, and their tech-savvy sister Darcy—who'd started Treasure Hunter Security together. Now Carter worked security for them.

She closed the file. The man also had an engineering degree, owned his one-bedroom condo in LoDo in Denver, and enjoyed snowboarding and the ladies. He apparently didn't keep any particular woman around for very long.

She hoped to hell he was more loyal to his

partners in the field than he was to the women he dated.

Elin packed up and headed out the door. She was meeting Hale at the FBI firing range in twenty minutes. As she jabbed the button for the elevator, her phone buzzed, and with a curse, she pulled it out to read the text.

A sharp pain sliced through her gut. It was from a friend back in DC. Apparently, her ex-husband had just gotten engaged.

Elin paused, staring blankly at the silver elevator doors. Barely a year since they'd signed their divorce papers, and Matthew was going to marry someone else.

She lifted her chin. Oh, she didn't miss Matthew. He'd taken master classes in passive-aggressive bullshit, and finally he'd given her an ultimatum—him or her job. She made a rude noise and shoved her phone back in her pocket. It had been an easy choice for her. Of course, he'd never do anything to jeopardize *his* career as a successful chef, but he'd expected her to adjust her work.

It had only taken two years of marriage for her to realize that she hadn't loved him. He'd just been a part of the plan she'd set for herself. Career, marriage, and eventually children. God, she hated herself a little to think Matthew had just been a box she could check off.

Now she had a revised plan. No men or relationships. She was focused on her career, and on nabbing her promotion. But she wouldn't lie to herself. The thought of Matthew remarrying, of making a life with someone else...it didn't make her jump for joy. *Maybe you're just jealous?*

Maybe, but she knew she needed to focus on what was important. If she completed this mission, she'd get what she'd been busting her butt for over the last two years. Hell, she'd been working hard since she was thirteen years old and Silk Road, still in its infancy, had stolen a painting her art restorer mother had been working on.

And killed Elin's father in the process.

She swallowed back old grief and was happy when the elevator dinged its arrival. She stepped inside and leaned against the wall. When her phone started to ring, she welcomed the distraction.

"Alexander." The elevator slowed.

"Hi, Elin."

She smiled and stepped out of the elevator. Caleb was a sexy lawyer she'd been dating casually back in DC. "Hi. You got my message."

"That you were heading out of town and didn't know when you'd be back."

His tone was cool and Elin winced. "I'm sorry. It's for work."

Caleb sighed. "I'd complain, if I hadn't had to cancel on our dates a lot as well. Pot and kettle, and all that."

That's why she thought they worked well. They caught up when they could, but didn't mind if the other had to reschedule. "I should be back in a few weeks."

"From where?"

"It's—"

"Classified," he finished with a sigh. "Look, Elin, you're smart and beautiful."

Her stomach took a nosedive. *Uh-oh.* "You're breaking up with me."

A pause. "Yeah. I've always been a workaholic, but you take it to the next level."

Elin strode out of the lobby. "Bad guys don't take evenings and weekends off, Caleb."

"I know. Look, dating you has made me see that I'm ready for something long term."

Her mouth tightened, and she stared up at the clear, blue Denver sky. "And that's not me?"

"That's not you."

"So I've been told before." Ahead sat the nondescript door heading into the warehouse that housed the firing range. "Look, Caleb, I have a meeting to get to. A classified one."

"I'm sorry, Elin. Goodbye."

She stabbed a finger at the phone and headed into the range. She was pretty sure the universe had it out for her today. *Let's make sure Elin knows she really sucks at relationships.*

Looking up at the long lanes set up for shooting, the scent of propellant from fired guns hit her, and she smiled sharply. She still had ten minutes until Hale Carter arrived. She was really in the mood to shoot something.

***

Hale gunned his Triumph and slid into a parking

spot in front of the nondescript warehouse in Stapleton. He kicked down the stand and pulled off his helmet.

Damn, she'd purred like a wildcat for him today. It had helped him shake off the cobwebs of a bad night's sleep. His jaw tightened and he swung off the bike. He wasn't thinking of the nightmares he couldn't seem to shake. They'd fade. Eventually.

He took a deep breath. After this mission, he might have to take a long ride up into the mountains and really test out his new toy. Cal had talked him into upgrading his bike, and so far, he wasn't disappointed.

Of course, now that Cal Ward was attached to a certain sexy photographer, he didn't seem quite as interested in all his adrenaline-fueled toys and activities. Hale didn't blame the guy. Dani was pretty awesome.

Not that Hale wanted a woman of his own. Nope. He pushed open the door to the FBI firing range. All his colleagues were falling in love left, right, and center. Hale was doing everything he could to avoid that particular bullet. He liked his life just the way it was.

Right now, he had a mission to think about.

He walked over to a counter to check in with the agent there. Adrenaline spiked in his blood. There was nothing Hale liked more than that sense of anticipation before a mission. Sure, they were no longer in war zones and under fire, but his expeditions with Treasure Hunter Security were almost always interesting. And on this one, he'd still get to nail the bad guys.

But there was one other thing that had him anticipating this mission. A certain cool, blonde FBI agent who would be accompanying him.

The agent behind the counter slid something across the scarred surface. "Hearing protection. Lane Ten," the agent told him. "Agent Alexander is waiting for you."

Hale took the earmuffs. "Thanks."

Several suited agents were in the range, firing different weapons. He looked around with interest. It was a good setup. A few standard lanes with paper targets, and a few with what looked like a high-tech electronic system. He itched to take a closer look.

Suddenly, he heard the distinctive sound of a M4 firing. Hale's footsteps faltered, and he barely stopped himself from flinching.

It was the preferred weapon of the SEALs.

Memories tried to crowd in, and like he always did, he shoved them back ruthlessly. He dragged in a deep breath. The past was the past. It was done, gone, and he couldn't change it.

His gaze snagged on a long, blonde ponytail.

He slowed to watch Elin firing. She was holding a Glock 23 handgun. Her stance was perfect, and she didn't flinch or jerk.

She finished firing and lowered her weapon. She pressed a button and her target zoomed in closer, running on a wire.

All the holes were centered around the crosshairs on the chest of the person-shaped target.

Except for one perfect shot right in the center of the forehead.

God, she was good *and* a badass.

"You're good."

She turned and pulled her earmuffs down around her neck. "I know."

Hale tried not to smile. She wasn't very tall, but her confident manner made her seem taller. She was wearing a sharp pantsuit, and he appreciated that the trousers gave him a decent view of compact curves. Her face was attractive, and combined with her gold-tinged skin, bright-blue eyes, and blonde hair, she made an impact. Add the gun and her confident posture, and she made him think of a Valkyrie.

"Your balance is slightly off," he said. "Not by much. But if you move a little more of your weight forward, you'll counteract the kick of the gun even better than you do now."

She calmly reloaded her weapon. "Why should I take your advice? Because you have a penis?"

Hale pressed his tongue to his teeth. "No. Because I used to be a Navy SEAL, and carried a weapon every day."

"Right, your big, bad SEAL credentials." She raised a brow. "I'm guessing you manage to slip that into most conversations, especially when you're chatting up pretty young things at bars."

Well, yeah. "Most women find it interesting and intriguing."

Her brow rose higher. "I work around men who carry guns all day long. Takes more than that to impress me."

Your balls have officially been busted, Carter. And he still wasn't turned off. The more Elin Alexander talked, the more intrigued he was.

Suddenly, she stepped closer and the scent of her hit him—fired gun and cool water. Now, why would that combination appeal to him so much?

She held out a gun to him. "Impress me."

He took the Glock, a twin to hers. "I prefer a SIG Sauer." He pulled his ear protection on, and stepped up to the line.

She touched something and several targets popped up. He realized it wasn't a simple, stationary target, but multiple moving ones. She was really testing him.

Hale let himself fall into the zone. It was a place he'd learned to find before a mission. Before he'd leaped out of a plane, rappelled out of a helicopter, or dived off a boat.

He squeezed the trigger, taking his shots, moving steadily.

Bang. Bang. Bang.

As he learned the weapon, he adjusted his grip and balance.

Bang. Bang. Bang.

The targets stopped, and he lowered the gun. They all popped back up. Every target had a single shot through the chest.

He pushed his ear protection off and smiled at her. Her gaze dropped to his mouth for a millisecond, and she blinked her cool, blue eyes. Then her gaze met his again.

"Are you going to tell me 'I told you so?'" she asked.

"Nope. A gentleman doesn't boast when he kicks ass. Even one as fine as yours, Agent Alexander."

She snorted. "Come on then, Mr. Carter. Let's discuss our mission."

"You got it, partner."

He got another cool look. Oh yeah, Hale was excited for this mission. And knowing he was headed into the desert with Special Agent Elin Alexander by his side just made it all the more stimulating.

Chapter Two

Elin led Hale into a small break room off the main firing range. She sat in a chair at the battered coffee table, while Carter settled his six-feet-three-inches of hard-packed muscle onto the couch opposite her.

He was a big man, but didn't move like one. No, he had a fluid, athletic grace, and added to that outrageously handsome face, he sure packed more of a punch than his photograph.

Okay, so the guy was good looking. She was an FBI agent...she was trained to notice these things.

He lifted his head and saw her watching him. He smiled, and Elin's breath caught in her throat. That gorgeous, panty-melting, brain-fuzzing smile had caught her before. It had the power to make a woman's brain go blank.

Note to self: when Hale Carter smiles, look away. He was like a solar eclipse.

Elin cleared her throat, keeping her voice businesslike. "As you know, we're planning to meet in Cape Town with the rest of the Silk Road team. From there, we'll head north to the Kalahari." She leaned forward. "My cover name is Alex Elliott. You'll be Carter Jordan. I figured we'd keep it close enough to our real names as possible to avoid any slip-ups."

Carter lifted his chin. "I won't slip-up."

"You know I've been undercover with this Silk Road cell." Months of burrowing deeper, and trying to gain their trust. It didn't matter that some days she felt the scum clinging to her, it would be worth it to see this mission through, and drive a hard blow at Silk Road. "When we needed extra muscle on this expedition, I brought your name up. The story is that we've worked together in the past, and I vouched for you with the expedition leader, Claude Renard. So, if you screw up, we'll both take the fall."

Carter's handsome face had turned serious, and he absorbed the words with a nod. "Tell me about Renard."

Elin turned her phone over and showed him a picture. Renard was a thin man with a narrow, intense face, large, dark eyes, and a scar down his left cheek.

"He's mean and short-tempered, but smart and organized. While we're on this trip, I need you to follow my lead."

Carter's eyebrows rose. "You want me to follow along like a good little doggie?"

She shot him a narrowed look. "No. I know you're good at your job, or Declan Ward wouldn't have recommended you. But this is my investigation, and I need to know that if I give you an order, you'll follow it."

"Is that how you treat all men in your life, Agent

Alexander? Sorry, Alex." He rested his long-fingered hands on his jeans-clad thighs. "You give them orders and expect them to jump?"

Her ex had accused her of something similar. She lifted her chin. "You just do as I say, and we won't have any problems."

"Oh, I think there'll be problems." Carter graced her with one of his million-dollar smiles. "But don't worry, Alex. I'll assess each and every situation, and if your orders are what's the best course of action, I'll follow them and have your back. That's what being partners is all about."

"Partners?"

"That's why I'm here. To work with you."

He had the faintest drawl that Elin was sure sent women into convulsions. "Look, I think—"

"I think it's time you tell me exactly what we're looking for out in the desert."

Elin stared at him. "Ever heard of the Lost City of the Kalahari?"

Hale frowned. "I didn't think there were any cities—lost or otherwise—in the Kalahari."

"I didn't either, but Silk Road thinks there is. Once we get to Africa, I'll update you on—"

A strong hand gripped her wrist, and her gaze shot back to his.

"Elin, we need to know everything. You want THS on standby as backup in case of an emergency. You want me by your side to help, not just be a bodyguard who'll follow orders."

Intelligence shone in the man's eyes, and she realized she'd underestimated him. She'd expected the muscles, the skills in the field, and someone who was good under fire. What she hadn't expected was Hale Carter.

She blew out a breath. "Fine. I'll share what I can. I'll email you a file about the Lost City." Elin glanced at her watch and stood. "I have another meeting to get to…"

"Let me guess, you're never late."

"No."

"You ever just kick back and loosen up a bit?"

She glared at him. "No. I'll see you in Africa, Mr. Carter."

He winked at her. "Count on it, Agent Alexander."

***

She was a beauty.

Hale leaned over the desk, tightening up the last of the screws. He lifted the grappling gun, settling it in his hands.

It was his best work yet.

He'd used big, bulky grappling guns in the Navy, but since he'd started at THS, in his free time, he'd been working on creating more compact versions. He'd tested his first prototype in the Amazon, on a mission to save the brother of Sydney Granger—who was his buddy Logan's girlfriend—from Silk Road. It had worked well. The elegant blonde had also tamed wild, grumpy Logan, and now ruled the business side of the THS office with her slim fist.

This new version of the grappling gun was even

lighter and smaller than his first. Darcy and Sydney had even bullied him into applying for a patent, and then conned Dec into showing it to a few of his military contacts.

Hale had always been more interested in fiddling with engines and electronics, than trying to sell any of his gadgets. Just like his mechanic mother, who still liked to tinker in the workshop his dad had built for her. His parents were another couple who were head over heels for each other.

He ran a hand down the grappling gun. This little beauty was all he needed, and she was coming with him into the Kalahari Desert. He also had some experimental grenades he'd been working on, and a shirt made from a high-tech, anti-ballistic fabric that performed better than Kevlar and looked no different than a regular shirt.

His gaze fell to the satellite maps spread out on the table before him. They all showed images of the Kalahari. It was one hell of a desolate place.

The red sands covered most of Botswana, and parts of Namibia and South Africa. He knew its name came from a local word meaning "a waterless place." He ran his finger over the snaking line of a dry riverbed. As a SEAL and with THS, he'd spent his fair share of time in the desert. Apart from the Okavango Delta to the east, this one looked as barren as they came.

Beneath him, the yacht rocked a little, and he looked out the cabin window. His gaze met the magnificent view of Table Mountain overlooking the lively city of Cape Town. Today, the flat-topped mountain was missing its famous tablecloth of cloud, the sky behind it bright and blue.

Outside, the busy waterfront was bustling with activity. There were hotels, apartment buildings, restaurants and a large shopping center beyond. Cape Town was one of his favorite cities in the world, but in just a few short days, he'd be leaving civilization behind. His jaw tightened. Just him, Elin Alexander, and a bunch of notorious black-market antiquities thieves. Fun.

Hale heard the creak of floorboards behind him. He froze, instincts flaring.

His SIG Sauer P226 was resting on the desk, the pistol just out of reach. His fingers flexed on his unloaded grappling gun, and he set it down. Instead, he curled his right hand around his coffee mug. Hale didn't need a gun to take down an attacker.

He spun, flicking the mug at the person sneaking up on him.

The woman dodged her head to the side, and smacked the cup away with amazing reflexes. The mug smacked into the wall and fell onto the cabin's rug, the cold remains of his coffee soaking into the plush pile.

Hale stood and thrust his hands on his hips. "What the hell, Morgan? You know better than to sneak up on me."

His Treasure Hunter Security colleague shot him a wry smile and shrugged. Morgan Kincaid was tall, toned, and lethal. Short, black hair feathered around an angular face, dominated by aqua-blue eyes. "I was just testing to see if you were on your game." She snatched up the mug and set it back on the desk. "Can't have you going soft when you're about to embed yourself with scum."

He scowled at her, well aware she was just jerking his chain. "I am *not* going soft."

"Besides, you're always tricky to sneak up on." She shoved her hands in her pockets. "It's good practice."

"If you want to practice your sneaking skills, try Coop." Hale was pretty sure Ronin Cooper was born sneaky. The man hadn't met a shadow he couldn't hide in or a target he couldn't sneak up on.

Morgan snorted. "I can't sneak up on Coop. The man is too good." Her mouth tipped into the closest Morgan would ever come to a pout.

While she dressed up under duress, Morgan preferred her cargo pants, guns, and knives to dresses and jewelry. She'd passed the rigorous BUD/S SEAL training, but when the Navy hadn't allowed her to join the teams, she'd left. That's when Declan Ward had snapped her up for Treasure Hunter Security.

A year ago, Hale had also accepted Dec's offer to join the team. It had been the lifeline Hale had needed. That he'd made good friends at THS, like Morgan, was an added bonus.

She wandered over and pressed a hip to the desk. "When are you going to make me a grappling gun like this?" She pressed a finger to the dull grey metal.

"When I've worked out all the kinks, and you ask me nicely."

She grinned, then her gaze shifted. "You're studying satellite images?"

He nodded. "I wanted to get a feel for the land and what's out there."

"Not much, by the looks of things." Morgan raised her head. "I came down to let you know Dec and Coop are out on the deck. There's a call from Darcy, and she has some information about the expedition."

Hale nodded and followed Morgan upstairs. Dec's sister was co-owner of Treasure Hunter Security, along with her brothers. While Dec and Cal, both former SEALs, did the field work, Darcy ran the tech side of the business back in Denver, and was a whiz with computers. Whatever information they needed, Darcy could find it. Whatever supplies they needed in the field, Darcy could organize it. And whenever they needed a rescue, Darcy coordinated sending in the cavalry.

Hale and Morgan climbed up the steps, and into the bright sunshine spilling across the deck of the sleek yacht. He looked over and saw two tall, broad-shouldered men standing by the railing.

Dec and Ronin were the same height. Dec was a little broader through the shoulders, and the lines around his mouth said he smiled more. Coop didn't smile much, and had a dark intensity that pumped off him.

Hale was happy to call both men friends and work mates. It wasn't just that the men were good at their jobs, but Hale felt a deeper connection. Like him, he knew both men had done things they wanted to bury and forget. Thankfully, Dec had given them a job where they could still use the skills they were good at—shoot, fight, and take down the bad guys.

"Where's Cal?" Hale asked.

"Talking with some local contacts about a helicopter."

Hale grinned. "Probably squeezing in some skydiving, while he's at it."

Dec lifted his head, his hair, a few weeks past needing a haircut, brushing his collar. He waved them over to where he was propping a tablet with a heavy-duty cover up on the outdoor table. He turned it so they could all see.

Darcy Ward's face filled the screen. She was easy on the eyes, that was for sure. As always, her dark hair was styled in a sleek cut that touched her jawline. Today, she was wearing a tailored blue shirt that made her blue-gray eyes look more blue than usual.

"Hi, everyone." Darcy waved. "How's Africa?"

"Cooling off, thankfully," Hale answered. Darcy was sitting in the offices of Treasure Hunter Security back in Denver. While Colorado was shaking off the snow and the plants were blooming, here in southern Africa, the summer was giving way to the fall. No one wanted to be headed into the desert in the middle of summer.

"Where's my fiancé?" Dec asked.

"Out at a dress fitting." Darcy smiled. "You'll be

23

pleased to know the wedding plans are progressing nicely."

Dec held up a hand. "Layne and I have a deal. I don't have to pick flowers or try cake. All I have to do is get myself to the wedding on the right day wearing a tux."

Hale covered his smile. Dec and Layne had fallen in love on a mission in Egypt and had been engaged ever since. A few weeks ago, they'd suddenly decided they didn't want to plan a huge wedding and wait another year to tie the knot.

Darcy snorted. "It's only a few weeks away, dear brother. You'd better hope Silk Road doesn't keep you in Africa any longer than planned."

"Then how about we get to work?" Dec suggested.

"I've been busy pulling together all the information I can for this expedition," she said.

"What have you got?" Dec crossed his arms over his chest.

"So, as you know, Silk Road is heading into the Kalahari Desert. Up until now, the FBI—" Darcy said the acronym like it tasted bad "—have been playing their cards close to their chests. But Agent Alexander sent through some data to Hale before you left Denver. We know what Silk Road is after." Darcy paused dramatically.

Dec rolled his eyes. "Darce, can you quit the theatrics?"

The brunette pulled a face at her brother. "You've been spoiling my fun for thirty years now, Declan." But her face turned serious. "They're searching for the Lost City of the Kalahari."

Hale frowned. "Elin mentioned it, but I've never heard of it."

Darcy pushed her hair back behind her ears. "It all started with a tightrope walker and circus performer called the Great Farini."

Hale sank into one of the chairs around the table. "This should be interesting."

Darcy tapped on the screen, and some images appeared. Hale studied the picture of a man. It was an old photograph, and the man had a heavy beard and his hair parted severely down the middle.

"This is the Great Farini, born William Leonard Hunt in 1838. He was born in New York, but his family moved to Canada when he was young. He became obsessed with performing and acrobatics."

"He wanted to run away and join the circus?" Morgan said.

"Yes," Darcy said. "And that's what he did. He performed around the world."

"What the hell does a circus performer have to do with a lost city in an African desert?" Coop asked with a frown.

"Well," Darcy said, leaning forward. "Farini met several San people, formerly called Bushmen, who were 'on display' as part of a circus show." A look crossed her face. "It makes me sick to think of those poor people dragged from their homes and their land, and then put on show. The San people have called the Kalahari home for millennia. Rock art in the Kalahari Desert attributed to the San is over seventy thousand years old."

"And?" Dec prompted.

"It's rumored they told Farini about the 'Old Race' who lived in their lands before they dried up, and built huge cities that now lay ruined and empty."

"Wow," Morgan murmured.

"Farini and his son mounted an expedition, and Farini became the first foreigner to cross untraveled parts of the Kalahari." Darcy's blue eyes flashed. "He came back with a fabulous story of stumbling on the ruins of a lost city made of giant rocks. They even made sketches."

Images appeared on the screen, and Hale studied the sketches. Towers of giant, stacked stones, tumbled-down walls, and strange circles of rocks set into the ground.

Hale tapped a finger on the table. "I've been poring over satellite maps of the region, Darce. I didn't spot any lost cities."

Her face reappeared, and she nodded. "There have been dozens of expeditions over the years. No one's found anything conclusive. Theories of what Farini saw range from natural rock formations, to him being lost and on the other side of the continent and seeing the ruins of Great Zimbabwe, to his 'city' just being the remains of farms built by the locals."

"But Silk Road knows something that makes them believe otherwise," Dec said. "I know the bastards can have some pretty strange ideas at times, but generally, for them to throw money at an expedition, they have sound intel."

Darcy nodded. "I agree. But that's all I have." She huffed out a breath. "A certain incredibly annoying and unhelpful agent wouldn't give me anything else. I was informed that it was too *dangerous* to transmit the data." She sniffed. "Like anyone could hack my system."

Hale tried to hide a grin. Darcy's feud with Agent Alastair Burke was legendary. "Didn't Burke hack your system?"

Her gaze narrowed. "I've upgraded since then."

Dec scowled. "Burke wanted us in on this mission to provide his agent with backup. We need more than this if we're going to do that safely."

Darcy nodded and looked at Hale. "Burke said Agent Alexander will have more information for us."

Hale smiled. "Then it's lucky I'm meeting with Agent Alexander in—" he tipped his wrist over to look at his heavy-duty watch "—thirty minutes."

"Bring her back here," Dec ordered. "I want more information, or the op is off."

Hale nodded. "I'm on it."

Chapter Three

Elin strode along the sidewalk, her pace brisk. Energy flowed through her body, anticipation in her blood. She was finally on the ground in Africa, and eager to get this mission underway.

She'd just finished meeting with the local law enforcement in Cape Town. As an FBI agent, the chance to work outside the US didn't come up very often. But occasionally, on certain cases, it did happen. It meant working hand-in-hand with her local counterparts—in this case, the National Intelligence Agency. The local feds were more than happy for her to take the lead on this assignment.

She looked up, her gaze running over the formidable Table Mountain rising high above the city. She really liked Cape Town, with its natural beauty, cosmopolitan feel, and friendly people. She dodged around a group of musicians playing on the sidewalk, and headed toward the bar for her meeting.

Her excitement had nothing to do with seeing Hale Carter again.

A breeze rushed in off the harbor and caught her

hair. She took a deep breath of the salty air. Soon, she'd be headed into the desert and her months of undercover work would pay off.

She pushed open the door and stepped inside. She waited for her eyes to adjust to the gloom. At this time of day, there weren't too many people in the place. The establishment was barely one step ahead of seedy, and smelled of stale beer. She headed over to the bar.

Pulling herself onto a stool, she rested her arms on the scarred wooden bar and felt her skin stick. She hid a wince. "Coke, please."

The bartender had dark, glossy skin, and dark curls that fell down her back. The woman nodded and moved away to get Elin's drink.

Elin glanced at her watch. Hale should have been here by now. He was three minutes late. She tapped her fingers on the wood.

Someone slid into the chair to her left. "Hey there, gorgeous. Figured you were looking for some company."

She glanced at the man with the heavy South African accent. He had a square jaw that probably did okay with the ladies, but she didn't need her FBI training to see he liked drinking a little too much—his face was flushed, and he had broken capillaries around his nose. His blond hair, several shades darker than her own, had a messy, just-rolled-out-of-bed look.

"I'm not." When the bartender set her drink down, Elin pushed some money across the bar.

"Aw, come on, gorgeous. Women like you

shouldn't be alone."

She barely stopped herself from rolling her eyes. "Trust me, I'm perfectly fine. I suggest you order another drink and head back to whatever rock you crawled out from under."

"Now you're just playing hard to get."

She swiveled her head and shot him a frosty glare. "Better yet, give up the drinking. You'll live longer. And then, why don't you head off and think about believing a woman when she tells you something? I'm not interested."

The man's face twisted into an ugly sneer. He leaned forward menacingly.

Elin jabbed out with her elbow, catching him in the center of his chest. The man gasped for air, staring at her with wide eyes. He stumbled off the stool, grabbed his drink, and then scurried away.

"You should have just pulled out your Glock and shot him. Would've been more merciful." The masculine voice was deep and smooth, and held more than a hint of amusement.

Elin watched Hale slide his big body into the seat that her would-be admirer had just vacated. She gripped her glass. She'd forgotten the impact he made. Dressed in dark-brown cargo pants and a khaki shirt, and with a hint of scruff on his strong jaw, he was the definition of rugged adventurer.

"Now you know how I deal with unwanted trouble." She took a sip of her drink. "Welcome to Cape Town."

He smiled, and even though she thought she was prepared, it made her brain fuzz. Damn him for being so good-looking.

"Nice to see you again, Elin." He looked around. "Sorry, Alex."

Alex? Her code name, right.

The bartender re-appeared, and this time, her bored look was replaced by a wide smile. "Can I get you something? Anything?"

Carter turned his smile on the woman. "Coke. Thanks."

Elin barely avoided rolling her eyes. He clearly knew how to use that smile. The bartender was back in a flash, setting a coaster down and sliding Hale's drink across to him. Elin noticed that the woman had written her phone number on the coaster. The bartender gave Hale a wink and sauntered away.

"The day after tomorrow, Claude's planned for us to fly north to Upington," Elin said. "He has vehicles and supplies waiting for us there."

Hale's face turned serious. "I'm ready."

"The plan is for your THS team to stay on standby. If we get into trouble, we'll call them in."

Hale nodded.

"And, if we find the Lost City and can catch Silk Road in the act of stealing ancient artifacts, THS will come in with the local authorities and help us make the arrests. Burke has already organized that with the local NIA and the Namibian Central Intelligence Service. I've just come from some meetings with the locals. They have bigger issues to deal with than stolen antiquities, so they've been happy for us to take the lead on this."

"And happy to claim any valuable antiquities or treasures that we find in the process."

She smiled. "Right."

"What's Silk Road looking for in the desert, Elin?"

"I told you—"

He leaned closer, and she got a hint of a woodsy cologne and man. "We both know they aren't looking for blocks of stone."

"I can't divulge—"

"Bullshit." He crossed his arms. "You want my help, you tell me what I need to know. If you tell me it's classified, I'm out the door."

She huffed out a breath. Annoying man. "Okay, Carter. Where are you staying?"

"THS has a yacht down at the marina."

She slid off her stool. "I'll brief you on everything I'm authorized to tell you." When his mouth opened, she held up a hand. "I promise to tell you everything relevant to the mission."

He studied her for a second, then nodded. "Well, Alex, looks like you and I are going for a stroll by the water."

***

Hale walked side-by-side with Elin, and kept sneaking looks at her.

Her tight, compact body was currently clothed in cargo pants and a white T-shirt. He tried not to notice how the shirt clung to her deliciously full breasts. Her face was pretty intriguing too, and she hadn't bothered with much makeup. Her blonde hair glinted in the sunlight, and was once again pulled up in a tight ponytail that drove him crazy with the way it swung from side to side.

Yes, he was intrigued by the interesting and efficient Special Agent Elin Alexander. There was a part of him that just wanted to muss her up a little. To see what she looked like when she let go and got a little flustered.

"Which way?"

Her cool tone snapped Hale out of thoughts that were rapidly heading for X-rated. He cleared his throat. "That's the yacht over there." He nodded his head, so that to any bystanders, it would look like they were just having a casual conversation.

Elin made a show of looking across the entire marina. But he knew she'd have memorized the yacht's location, dock number, and all exits.

Suddenly, her body stiffened. She spun and linked her arm through Hale's.

He frowned down at her. "What's going on?" He kept his voice to a murmur.

"I think we have some company." She tapped his arm, and he saw she was pointing off to the left.

That's when Hale spotted the man. He was a big guy, one dock over from the THS yacht. He was sitting on a bench, a newspaper in his lap that was barely covering a pair of heavy-duty binoculars. He was staring at the yacht.

"Shit." Hale pulled out his phone and thumbed the speed dial.

Declan's deep voice answered. "Ward."

"Dec. We have company watching the yacht."

Dec cursed.

"Elin and I will take care of it," Hale said.

"Do it. Bring them in for a chat." The call cut off.

"Ready?" Hale asked Elin as they headed toward the man, strolling like a happy couple.

She leaned into him and smiled. "If Silk Road is onto us and they blow our cover…"

Yeah, he knew what it meant. If Silk Road got wind that either the FBI or THS was onto their expedition, they'd disappear so fast that heads would spin.

Or Hale and Elin would end up dead.

Elin leaned into him, those tantalizing breasts brushing against him. She let out a low laugh and the sound speared through him.

Shit, Hale. Focus.

The man had long, black hair pulled back in a tail at the base of his beefy neck. He gave them a quick glance, and then looked away, unconcerned.

Big mistake. *Big* mistake.

As they reached the man, Elin slipped her arm away from Hale's. A second later, Hale lunged forward, slamming a punch into the man's face.

The man flew sideways, falling off the bench. His binoculars clattered on the ground.

But he recovered fast. He leaped to his feet, raising his fists like a boxer. He launched a fist at Hale. Hale dodged, and slammed an uppercut into the man's gut. He groaned and staggered, and Hale landed another punch to the man's head, snapping it back.

Elin moved, landing a kick in the man's back. He went down on his knees, and she jerked the man's arms up behind his back. She eyed Hale. "Nice moves."

"You too."

A faint smile turned her lips up. As she pulled out a zip tie, Hale really wanted to know what she looked like when she smiled outright.

The Silk Road idiot decided to make a last-ditch attempt to escape.

He threw his head back, aiming for Elin. He rammed into her arms and she grunted. The man wrenched his arms free and bounded to his feet. He spun and started running.

Elin took two steps and jumped on the man's back. She rode him down to the ground. His face hit the concrete, blood spurting from his nose. He yelped and, lightning fast, she yanked his wrists together and tied them.

She stood, dusting her hands off.

Hale stared at her. "I think I'm in love."

She gave him a look. "Maybe you're coming down with something. I'm sure it'll pass."

Hale leaned down and grabbed a handful of the man's shirt. He yanked him up.

The guy was making horrible wet noises, blood covering his face. "See thuckin' roke my ose!"

"Come on, my friend." Hale spun the man around. "We'll get you tidied up, and then it's time for a chat."

"Thuck you!"

"You don't want to cooperate." Hale shrugged.

"Then I'll be happy to let her spend a bit more time with you."

The man stiffened and went silent. As they neared the yacht, Dec and Coop appeared out of the shadows. Dec glanced at the man and then at Elin and Hale. With a nod, he led them up the ramp onto the yacht.

"Nice to see you again," Elin said to Declan, not using names.

Dec lifted his chin. "You, too."

Hale shoved the man across the deck, and pushed him into a chair.

"This is interesting." Elin yanked up the man's sleeve. A circular tattoo was inked on his bicep. It held the silhouette of a camel with mountains behind it. "Symbol of Silk Road."

Dec muttered a curse. "How did you find us?"

The man's jaw tightened and he looked out to sea.

"I can get him to talk," Coop said in a quiet, scary voice.

The man's gaze darted to Coop, and he shifted uneasily.

Elin jerked her head to the opposite side of the deck. Leaving Coop to guard the man, Dec, Hale and Elin huddled.

"I can't let you guys deal with him," Elin said quietly.

Hale rounded on her. "What? We need to know what he knows—"

"I need to call my local contact at the NIA. I'm handing him over to them for questioning."

Hale crossed his arms over his chest. "He won't talk to them."

"He probably won't talk at all," Elin said. "The main thing is he didn't recognize either you or me when we approached him. Our cover hasn't been blown."

Hale heaved out a disgruntled breath. "Agreed."

"I'm calling the NIA now." She pulled out her phone. "When they arrive, you hand him over to them."

Dec didn't look happy, but he finally nodded.

"Besides, they might take a little bit of time to get here." Elin gave them a cool smile.

Hale laughed. God, she was something.

Dec smiled back and looked at Coop. "I think we'll keep our guest company until then."

Elin nodded and looked at Hale. "We have a mission brief to go over."

Hale waved a hand into the main cabin. "After you." She strode ahead of him and he watched that golden hair swing against her back.

Morgan and Cal looked up from a built-in couch inside. They were eating grilled sandwiches.

"Hey," Morgan said.

"Morgan, Cal, this is Special Agent Elin Alexander. Morgan Kincaid and Callum Ward."

Elin shook hands with Morgan and then Cal, who was almost a carbon-copy of Dec with bluer eyes and a readier smile. Then Elin looked down at the satellite maps and the printout of old photos and sketches from Farini's expedition laid out on the glossy wooden table. "You've been busy."

"I have." Darcy's voice came from the tablet nearby.

"I've heard good things about your skills, Ms. Ward," Elin said.

"Darcy, please. And I wouldn't trust *anything* Agent Burke tells you."

Elin raised a brow. "He's my boss."

"My commiserations. Now, are we ready to discuss this expedition?"

"Yes." Dec strode in. "Coop's having a chat with our *friend*. Hale's the lead on this one, I'll let him do the talking, but Elin...we need to know everything. I won't risk my man, or try and provide back up without knowing what we're dealing with. Burke's always been straight with me."

A snorting noise came from the tablet.

"The guy talk?" Hale asked.

Dec scowled. "No."

Hale stepped closer to Elin. He could smell her perfume—that same freshwater smell that made him think of a cool mountain lake. "Why is Silk Road interested in some old rumor about the Lost City of the Kalahari? We don't think a pile of old rocks would interest them much."

Elin looked at them all. "It isn't about the Lost City itself...it's about what the Lost City really is."

Hale felt the air in the cabin charge. "Go on."

Elin clasped her hands behind her back. "Farini kept journals documenting his trip to the Kalahari. When he returned to London, he published several books, and even held public talks in London about his expedition. Strangely, he recorded very little about his discovery of the Lost City of the Kalahari."

"He was keeping it a secret," Hale said.

Elin nodded.

"He was planning to come back and exploit something at the city himself?" Hale continued.

"That would be my best guess," Elin said.

"But what?" Darcy asked.

"Silk Road got its hands on a previously unseen journal of Farini's. It appears the man was spending a lot of time with a Mistress Strange, an occultist who worked at his circus. She recognized some symbols that Farini saw carved on the rocks of his Lost City."

Hale leaned forward. Elin was so matter-of-fact in her delivery, he wondered if she felt the same intense curiosity to uncover, the electric charge that made him want to solve a mystery. Or was this just a job for her?

When she turned her head and their gazes met, he suppressed a smile. Oh yeah, she felt it. Her eyes glittered, and he knew Elin wasn't as cool and composed as she acted.

"What were the symbols, Elin?" Hale asked.

"They were a pentagram inside a circle, and the symbol of two closed, interlinked loops."

Darcy gasped. "The Star of David and Solomon's Knot. Symbols of King Solomon."

Murmurs filled the cabin.

"Wait." Dec held up a hand. "The King Solomon from the Bible?"

"That's the one," Elin said.

"So," Hale said. "You're saying that Silk Road believes that the Lost City of the Kalahari is linked to King Solomon?"

"Ever heard of Ophir?" Elin asked.

The name tweaked something in Hale's head, but he couldn't remember what.

"Ophir?" Morgan said, straightening. "I've heard Zach mention it recently."

Morgan's boyfriend was a history professor, who worked at the Denver Museum of Nature and Science.

"Ophir was mentioned in the Bible," Morgan said. "Every three years, the Kingdom of Ophir sent a shipment of gold, diamonds, ivory and other treasures to King Solomon."

Cal let out a whistle. "Sounds like quite a haul for those times."

"Wait a second." Dec turned to stare at Elin. "Are you talking about King Solomon's Mines?"

Morgan grinned. "I love that movie."

Elin's nose screwed up. "We aren't talking about low-budget adventure movies. King Solomon received gold and other valuables from somewhere."

"There are all kinds of speculations on where Ophir might have been located," Darcy said, the sound of tapping keyboard keys punctuating her words. "In Arabia, in North Africa, in southern Africa. Hell, the Solomon Islands in the Pacific are named for Solomon, and the belief that Ophir was an island nation."

Hale shifted. "But Silk Road believes that Ophir

is the Lost City of the Kalahari?"

"Yes," Elin said. "We all know that southern Africa is riddled with gold and diamond mines. It makes sense."

"So they're after old gold and diamond mines?" Dec shook his head. "Even if they discover it, whatever country the mines are located in, the government will notice and boot Silk Road out. It's got to be more than that."

Hale watched the minute expressions on Elin's face. "There's treasure."

Elin shot him a look. "Yes. There's treasure."

"Fuck," Dec cursed.

Hale knew how Dec felt. Treasure tended to make things a lot more volatile and dangerous. "What is it?"

"I don't know."

"Bullshit," Dec said. "I'm not taking my team in blind."

Elin shoved her hands in her pockets. "I'm not lying. Claude hasn't trusted me with the information. The man is paranoid. From the snooping I've managed to do, it is some sort of treasure linked to King Solomon."

"I'll start running some searches," Darcy said.

"I wish I had more for you," Elin said. "And as soon as I do, I'll pass it on."

Dec ran a hand through his hair. "Fine. Hale will be with you on the expedition. The plan is for me, Coop, Cal, and Morgan to fly into Windhoek in Namibia. We'll wait for you there with a chopper on standby. If you need backup, you call us." Dec's gaze landed on Hale. "Don't take any risks, Hale."

"How will we be able to contact you?" Elin asked. "We can't risk a sat phone or something that Silk Road can trace. And conventional phones aren't going to work out in the desert."

Hale smiled. "Leave that to me."

"Oh?"

Dec smiled. "Hale's our resident gadget man."

Elin eyed Hale. "You're full of surprises."

He grinned at her, his lips twitching. He wanted to say something suggestive, but with all his friends around him, he bit his tongue. Besides, he didn't want to end up on the floor with his hands zip-tied.

As Dec and Elin ironed out some more logistics, Hale looked at the maps and photos on the table. Red-orange sand dominated the images, and for a second, he flashed back to another unforgiving desert, one that had chewed him up and spat him out. One that had taken his fellow SEALs.

Hale shifted so fast, he knocked over a chair. He grabbed it and righted it.

Elin turned his way. "I have to go. So, I'll see you the day after tomorrow."

"I look forward to it."

After nodding at the others, she spun and walked out. She had a stride that warned she was a woman on a mission, and not to get in her way.

"Better not step out of line, Hale," Morgan murmured with a grin. "Or Agent Alexander will show you who's boss."

Hale fought back a smile.

Cal snorted. "Something tells me the man might enjoy that."

"Enough." Hale headed down the stairs to the lower level. "I have some prep work to do." He wanted to check his gear. He needed to test out the small comms patch he'd developed, and finish up with his grappling gun.

"Pizza for dinner," Morgan yelled. "It was Dec's turn to cook, so I decided to save us from a bout of food poisoning."

"I sign your paychecks, remember, Kincaid," Dec growled.

In his cabin, Hale pulled out one of the small, experimental comms patches. It was no bigger than his thumbnail, and as thick as a few layers of skin. It was satellite-linked, and used bone conduction technology to send and receive audio via vibrations through the skull. He'd designed the little sucker to stealthily piggy-back off any existing satellite tech in range.

He hadn't had a chance to test it in the field...so this mission was a test run combined with the real thing. Shit, he hoped it worked.

Sitting at his desk, he touched the clear patch. It was designed to go behind his ear and when activated, he'd be able to communicate with the THS team in Windhoek. He pulled out his small travel toolkit, unwrapped his tools, and set to work.

When he finally raised his head, his neck was stiff, and outside, night had fallen. He realized his left hand ached, and he looked down at his little finger. It sat at a twisted angle and was covered in scar tissue.

It was a daily reminder of what he'd survived. What the insurgents had done to him and his fellow SEALs: Sean, Dutch, Clem, Chris, and Shep. Hale blew out a breath. So he'd been tortured? So he saw his buddies in his dreams every night? He'd survived and his friends hadn't. He flexed his deformed finger and shook his head. He needed to focus on his latest mission.

His cellphone rang. Frowning, he picked it up and saw that Elin was calling.

He smiled, but only for a second. For the ever-efficient Agent Alexander to be calling him, it meant something was wrong.

Chapter Four

"Miss me?"

Elin listened to Hale's smooth drawl through the line. It was wrong for one man to be so attractive. "There's been a change of plans. Claude wants to leave first thing in the morning."

A pause. "Why?"

"My guess? He was waiting for our long-haired friend that we handed over to the NIA to check in." And now the man was missing, and it had spooked Claude. "He's hired a private jet. He wants the team on it so we can take off at dawn. We'll fly to Upington and from there, we take four-wheel-drives into the desert."

She heard Hale mutter a curse. She could practically hear his thoughts turning over.

"Okay, I'll meet you at the airport in a few hours," he said.

"See you there."

Elin packed up her bags and tried to grab a little sleep. Instead, she tossed and turned in her hotel bed. There was a mix of excitement, anticipation, and edginess in her veins that refused to let her relax. When her alarm went off, she had what she knew might be her last decent shower for a while, dressed, then snatched up her Glock and slipped it into the holster at the small of her back. She grabbed her duffel bag, and headed to check out.

As her taxi drove toward the airport, the sun was just starting to rise. The leafy trees and modern city buildings gave way to open spaces, and in the distance, the edges of the slums. Buildings cobbled together from whatever the residents could find—bricks, sheets of iron, wood. A reminder that not everyone got to enjoy Cape Town's cosmopolitan flare.

As the rising sun turned the eastern horizon pink, Elin prayed that the mission would be a success. She wanted to bring down Silk Road, wanted to tell her mother that she'd finally dealt a blow to the group who'd destroyed their family. And she also wanted her promotion. It would be a...validation. Something that would make her broken marriage and failures in her personal life worth it.

They turned into the airport and she tightened her ponytail. She'd bring Silk Road down. She also wanted to protect the history out there, whatever it was they were hunting at Ophir. Silk Road didn't revere history, they destroyed and captured, and sold it all for profit.

Elin's mother had taught her the importance of history. Her earliest memories were of sitting at her mother's feet as Victoria Alexander worked to restore a painting. Her mother was one of the best art restorers in the world, with steady, capable hands and a patience Elin had always been in awe of.

So Elin wasn't going to let Silk Road pillage Ophir, and the mines of one of history's most famous kings. She wouldn't let them profit from King Solomon's treasure...or kill for it, either.

She paid her taxi driver and stepped out of the car. After a short walk and a flash of her papers at a sleepy-looking woman at the desk in the tiny terminal for private flights, Elin stepped out onto the tarmac.

A large shape emerged from the shadows near the building. She tensed, then relaxed. Hale.

Somehow, he looked scruffier and more dangerous than when she'd seen him a few hours ago. But no less attractive. Her belly fluttered, and she stomped on the reaction. Now was not the time.

He hid it under the charm and the smiles, but she knew he was dangerous. She'd watched him fight—with power and ease. She knew that there were solid muscles under his faded shirt. There were so many facets to Hale Carter and she wasn't exactly sure she'd worked him out yet.

"Morning," she said.

He fell into step beside her, a duffel bag similar to hers over his shoulder, as well as a large, black, battered backpack. She felt the heat radiating off his body.

"Sleep well?" he asked.

"Like a baby," she answered. "That's a lot of stuff."

"Never go on a mission without this." He patted his backpack.

"What's in there?"

"Climbing gear, prototype grappling gun, spare ammunition, and a few other little surprises I've put together."

"A regular bag of tricks. Everything legal in there?"

His smile flashed white in the darkness. "I plead the fifth."

"I don't want to know, Carter." As they neared the sleek jet on the tarmac, Elin spotted the small group waiting for them.

A man pushed forward. "Alex. I thought for once you might be late."

Elin felt Hale looking at her but focused on Claude. "I'm never late. This is Carter."

When she glanced at Hale, he had a hard look on his face. He looked like the perfect mercenary-for-hire.

Claude gave a little bow. "*Bonjour*. I'm Claude Renard. This is Sabine." He motioned at the tall, lean woman lounging on the steps of the jet. She had a cloud of bright-red hair piled messily on top of her head.

The woman took her time running her gaze down Hale's body. She shot him a lazy smile.

Elin didn't like Sabine, and the feeling was mutual. They'd had several prickly interactions, and the woman had made it clear that Claude and their work were her territory. Elin hadn't been able to find out anything about Sabine, not even her full name. But one thing was for certain, the woman wasn't just Claude's lover and right-hand woman...she was his bodyguard.

There were four others standing nearby. Three men and one woman who all screamed ex-military. Elin nodded at them. They were all part of Claude's cell and she'd worked with them over the last few months. "Carter Jordan. Rex, Westcott, Thompson and Van Wyk."

Hale lifted his chin but no one shook hands.

"We fly to Upington," Claude said. "It's the largest town on the Orange River to the north. I have vehicles and supplies organized." He shifted. He rarely stood still, a nervous energy continuously radiating off him. "From there, we head into the desert."

There were murmurs.

"And then we find what no one else has discovered." A light ignited in his dark eyes. "The lost city of Ophir." He let his gaze sweep over them all. "Let's go."

As the others headed up the steps, Claude's gaze settled on Hale.

"Don't mess up," Claude said. "I dislike messes, and Sabine dislikes cleaning them up for me."

"He's good, Claude," Elin said. "He's good under fire, and he's also good at fixing things."

Claude shoved his hands in his pockets, his face turning considering. "Okay. But he screws up, it's on you, Alex." A sharp smile. "And neither of you will like the consequences."

Elin shrugged, unconcerned. She'd seen him kill

one man in a rage, and another with a cold, calculated, point-blank shot to the head. Claude was dangerous and unpredictable, and she knew it would pay not to underestimate him.

"No one is screwing up." She strode up the steps, brushing past a smirking Sabine.

Elin ducked inside and moved toward the back of the jet. Large, plush armchairs in cream leather lined the interior. She sat down on one near the back.

A second later, Hale sat down beside her, crowding her. He was way too big. Her gaze lingered on where his T-shirt stretched over all those muscles.

She jerked her gaze forward and shifted in her chair, trying to get comfortable. "Ready?"

"Yep." He settled back in the chair and closed his eyes. "I'm always ready."

Cocky. Soon, everyone was settled and the jet was hurtling down the runway. Elin looked out the window, anticipation in her blood, even as she kept her face composed.

Showtime.

***

Hale stared out the aircraft window and saw the river appear below.

The Orange River was the longest river in South Africa, and looked like a snake of green through the harsh red-brown landscape. A geometric patchwork of irrigated farm fields lined the river.

Elin shifted, her shoulder bumping into him. She huffed out a breath. "Personal space, Carter."

He sat back in his seat, studying her face. Him being too close bothered her, huh? "Better get used to it, Alex. We're going to be sharing very close quarters for the next few weeks."

She looked out the window. They were approaching the town of Upington, nestled up against the northern side of the river.

"Farini came through here on his expedition," Elin said quietly.

"I bet it's a little different now." Hale lifted his gaze to the desert beyond. He guessed that part was still the same. The green surrounding the river ended abruptly, and beyond that, it was shades of brown, beige, and red as far as the eye could see. A few hundred kilometers to the north was the border with Botswana, and not too far to the north west was Namibia. If they did manage to find Ophir and Solomon's mines, it was anyone's guess what country it might lie in.

"There was a picture of Farini and his son overlooking a waterfall he called the Hundred Falls," she said. "It's called Augrabies Falls, now. If you follow the river west about a hundred kilometers, you'll reach it. The river drops over sixty meters into a magnificent gorge. Almost unchanged from when Farini sat beside it."

Her perfume tickled his senses. Even after two hours on the plane, she still smelled fresh. "Let's hope whatever Farini found out in the desert is still there, too." He turned his head to take another look at the rest of the group.

He didn't like the look of Claude. The man was edgy and jumpy, always running a hand through his hair, and jiggling a foot. Combine that with a lack of conscience, and it was never a good combination. The woman by his side, in contrast, rarely moved. Something about Sabine made Hale think of a snake lying in wait for prey. She was dangerous, no doubt about it.

The rest of the team members were clearly all ex-military. From the accents, three Americans and one South African.

Soon, the jet's wheels touched down, and they pulled into Upington's terminal. Hale grabbed his duffel bag and reached for Elin's.

She shot him an arch look.

"Just being a gentleman," he told her.

"Don't." She snatched her bag up herself.

Hale shook his head. Prickly, independent women had never really been his thing. He liked women who laughed a lot and enjoyed a good time. No strings, no mess, no fuss.

But for some reason, thorny and challenging was proving far too enticing.

As they shuffled off the plane, the warmth hit him. Summer had passed, but apparently someone had forgotten to tell the desert.

They followed Claude across the tarmac. The man was moving fast, Sabine's long legs keeping pace beside him. He led them out to where four rugged four-wheel-drives were parked in a row at the curb in front of the terminal. The beige Land

Rovers were kitted out for the desert, with gear stored on the roofs, including rooftop tents. Hale glanced in the back of one, and saw camping gear and large plastic bottles of water. He suspected the vehicles would all have long-range fuel tanks, as well.

"Sabine and I will take the lead vehicle," Claude announced. He patted the side of the Land Rover. "She's been specially outfitted just for me. Armor-plated, run-flat tires, reinforced suspension."

Clearly the rest of them didn't warrant the same protection. Hale hoped to hell they wouldn't need it.

"Rex and Westcott, you take the next one," Claude ordered with a wave. "Then Thompson and Van Wyk. Alex, you and your man bring up the rear."

"What's the rush?" Elin asked. "First you move up the timetable, and now we're heading straight out?"

The man's shoulders moved. Definitely twitchy.

"There are other players involved now. There's been a leak about our trip to the Lost City. I need to get there first, and claim what's mine."

"Other players?" Hale pulled his duffel bag up higher on his shoulder.

"The fucking FBI and their Art Crime Team." Claude shoved his hands on his hips, annoyance on his face. "And those Treasure Hunter Security bastards."

Hale barely controlled his jerk. How the fuck did he know? "Heard those THS guys are do-gooder pains in the ass."

"*Oui*," Claude agreed. "You are correct, Carter. The Wards are often in our way."

"But the FBI?" Hale said. "I thought they couldn't operate outside the USA."

"The prick that leads the Art Crime Team, an agent by the name of Burke, has *la trique*," Claude gesticulated wildly, "a hard-on for our organization. He is a dog nipping at the heels of Silk Road." Claude shook his head. "It is not like we are selling weapons or drugs."

Hale barely resisted looking at Elin. No, they were just selling history off piece by piece, and killing anyone who got in their way.

Claude scowled. "There's also someone else asking questions."

Hale looked at Elin now. She was frowning. "Who?" he asked.

"We don't know." The Frenchman chopped a hand through the air. "My sources have just said that someone has been asking questions. Someone who is after my treasure."

So there definitely was a treasure of some description. What the hell could it be?

Claude's dark eyes flashed. "I don't plan to let anyone beat me to Ophir. Now, let's take a look at our route and get moving."

Sabine handed Claude a map. He opened it up on the hood of the lead four-wheel-drive.

"Based off Farini's lost journal, what he found in the desert was actually an outpost of Ophir."

"Not the city itself?" Elin asked.

"Correct. And there is a clue at the outpost. A key that will lead us in the direction of the city and the mines."

Hale decided to take a risk. "What's this treasure? What's so special about it?"

Claude paused for a second. "Something beyond value, Mr. Jordan. Something that belonged to King Solomon himself." Claude folded up the map.

"King Solomon got treasure sent to him from the mines." Hale frowned. "Why would he send something valuable *back*?"

Claude stuck the map under his arm. "To hide it. Now, enough questions. Let's go."

Hale loaded his duffel bag into the back of his and Elin's Land Rover. As he slid into the driver's seat, Elin climbed into the passenger seat. He glanced curiously at her.

"You going to argue with me about driving?" he asked.

She shrugged. "You'll get bored of it eventually, and be begging me to drive later."

God, she was something, and she was probably right. Ahead, the rest of the convoy pulled out. Hale set the Land Rover in gear and followed.

He watched Elin pull a small device out of her pocket, and start waving it around the dash, the console, the ceiling. He recognized the tech straight away. He had a few of these little babies himself. She was checking for bugs.

As they drove out of Upington, she climbed into the back to finish her check. Finally, she climbed back into the passenger seat. "Clean."

"So, who do you think this mystery player is?"

"No idea. I'll send the info to Alastair when I can. My tablet has a satellite connection. I'm more worried about how much they know about the FBI and THS being involved."

Hale gripped the steering wheel, turning all the information over in his head. "What do you think about this treasure belonging to King Solomon?"

"It's what I expected," she said. "But I still don't know what it could be, or why it's so valuable."

Hale stared ahead as the desert spread out ahead of them. "I think we have a whole lot of questions, and not very many answers."

Chapter Five

Darcy Ward loved having the office to herself.

She set her cup of chai tea latte down beside her computer and pressed her finger to the fingerprint recognition pad to unlock her system.

Morning sunlight shone through the windows of the warehouse and she knew Sydney would be in soon. Logan O'Connor's smart, elegant girlfriend had taken over the business side of THS, for which Darcy was forever grateful.

She sipped her tea and studied the screens. She needed to check if her searches had found any more information on what treasure Silk Road could be after in the depths of King Solomon's Mines. Pausing, she stared ahead, wondering what it would be like to be out in the field, being the first person to step into the legendary mines after centuries.

Darcy wrinkled her nose. Unfortunately, she knew being in the field also meant heat, flies, bullets whizzing, and sleeping on the ground. Shaking her head, she tapped in some new searches. Give her an office any day.

The sound of the front door opening had her turning around with a smile.

But it wasn't Sydney Granger who'd arrived.

Darcy groaned. "What the hell are you doing here?"

Special Agent Alastair Burke, head of the FBI's specialized Art Crime Team, raised a dark brow. "Good morning, Darcy."

She scowled at the man. "It was."

"It's a pleasure to see you again," he added, his tone dry.

He was wearing a dark suit that did little to hide the fact that the man had a hard, muscled body. She was certain there was a rule that said FBI agents were supposed to be middle-aged, slightly overweight, and with thinning hair.

Her gaze moved up his not-overweight body to his neatly-cut, mahogany-brown hair. He shifted, resting a hand on his hip. It parted his jacket and she saw his holster and gun. A shot of heat hit her belly. Damn, why did men in suits with holsters look so sexy? It wasn't fair.

"Always so polite and welcoming," he said.

She pasted on a sweet smile. "Agent Burke, to what do I owe this unexpected pleasure?" *And how the hell do I get you out of here?*

His lips quirked. It was the closest she'd ever come to seeing him smile. "You didn't even choke when you said pleasure."

"Just tell me what I need to do to get you to turn around and head out the door."

Burke shook his head. "Sorry, I'm not planning

on leaving."

Her eyes widened. "What?"

The front door opened again and three more FBI agents—two men and a woman—entered. They were carrying laptops and file boxes.

A heavy feeling settled on her, and she stared into Burke's intense, green eyes. Damn, the man wasn't yanking her chain.

"With my agent in the field, along with your team, I decided it made sense to pool our resources on this mission."

"*You* decided," Darcy said.

"You want to do everything you can to help keep Hale and your brothers safe, don't you?"

She hissed out a breath. "Of course, I do."

He waved to the agents. "Then let my team plug in and share what we have. From here, we'll work together and coordinate everything the field team needs." Burke's face hardened. "And do whatever needs doing to bring Silk Road down."

Darcy huffed out a breath. She could hardly argue with any of that. "Fine." She nodded at the agents. "I'm Darcy Ward."

One by one, the agents introduced themselves.

Darcy pointed to some empty desks. "Help yourselves. Let me know if you need anything." She kept her face blank. "And I'll grant you access to my system."

Burke looked at her. "That won't be necessary. We can access the system ourselves."

Her gaze narrowed. "No, you can't."

He took a step toward her and she got a whiff of

his crisp, clean cologne. Damn him for smelling so good.

"Want to make a bet?" he said softly, so only she could hear.

Dammit, the man was far too smug. "You already got in."

This time, Special Agent Burke graced her with a full smile. She blinked. Holy hell, the man was gorgeous.

Get it together, Darcy. He's arrogant, annoying, bossy, and a thorn in your side, remember? "We work together to keep our people safe out there, but while you're here, you stay out of my way." She lifted her chin. *Take that, Agent Burke. Score one for Darcy.*

But Burke leaned closer, his voice low and silky. "What are you so afraid of, Darcy? Having me here, or finding out you like it?"

She stood there, frozen to the spot. Then he turned and walked over to his agents.

Dammit, she should have laughed. Scoffed. Made a witty comeback.

But right now, it appeared she was fresh out of witty comebacks. *Damn.* Score one for Agent Arrogant and Annoying.

***

"Don't you get sick if you read while you're in a car?" Hale asked.

Elin looked over at him. "No." She looked back down at the tablet. She was pulling up everything she could on King Solomon.

"Of course, you don't," Hale said. "You're the perfect Agent Alexander."

"Well, I aim for perfect. Aiming for mediocre is a waste of time."

Hale threw his head back and laughed. It was a deep, rich sound that made her stare at him. She also felt a gut-deep bolt of arousal.

No. Absolutely not. They were on a dangerous mission. She stared down at the tablet again, the screen blurring. She did not have the time to be attracted to the sexy, charming Hale Carter.

"What have you found on King Solomon?" he asked. "By now, I expect you to have it all organized and color-coded."

She shot him a cool look. "I prefer numerical coding. It makes it far easier."

Another laugh, and this time, Elin had to fight back a smile.

"I found some interesting articles about King Solomon. He was the wise and wealthy king mentioned in the Bible."

"I know the baby story," Hale said.

She smiled. "Right. Let's hope no babies actually got cut in half to settle disputes. He was the King of Israel, son of the famous David, of Goliath fame. He was also the builder of the famous temple. Most historians date his reign to around 950 BC. He was also known as an accomplished magician."

"Magic, huh?"

"Yes. Stories about him got entangled with the occult centuries later."

Hale nodded. "Any particular treasures linked to him?"

"Apart from all the gold, diamonds, ivory, and the other wealth he accumulated?"

"Right."

"Loads." She sighed. "The Ark of the Covenant. A magical throne. A golden table. A ring, and a key."

"Key?"

"Sounds like it was a magical book. The throne and table were made of gold, and magic as well. They were apparently looted by enemies. The ring was known as the Seal of Solomon, topped with the Star of David symbol, and was also—"

"Let me guess...magic."

"Ding, ding, you win the prize." She sat back in her seat. "It allowed Solomon to amass wealth and wisdom, and to control djinn."

"Djinn? Demons, right?"

"Genies. Supernatural beings of Islamic mythology. They were said to be able to travel instantaneously between locations, and Solomon was said to have used them to build his temple."

Hale grunted. "I like to believe there's a grain of truth in every myth and legend. On previous expeditions, I've seen some pretty crazy and amazing stuff."

"Yes, I've heard about some of your Treasure Hunter Security missions."

"So, we're on the hunt for either the Ark of the Covenant, a golden table, a golden throne, a book of spells, or a magic genie ring," he said.

"Sounds like it," she said. "Of course, they don't really have magical powers."

He raised a brow. "You don't believe in magic, Agent Alexander?"

"No. I'm a realist."

"Would never have guessed."

She wrinkled her nose at the sarcasm, but a bump in the road made them both jerk. The road was slowly getting rougher, and she knew it was only a matter of time before the pavement gave way to dirt. Elin went back to her research and they continued on.

"Look," Hale said.

Elin raised her head and spied a scraggly tree ahead. A male lion lounged in the scant shade. He watched them with a bored, lazy look as they drove past. She'd seen lions in the zoo before, but it didn't quite compare to seeing them in the wild. For a little while, the stark desert had made her forget just what called this land home.

Another hour passed, and Elin's prediction proved correct. Claude's vehicle led them onto the dirt, dust spewing up behind it.

"Getting close to the border with Botswana," Hale said.

But as they neared the border, Claude turned west, staying inside South Africa for now.

The land slowly turned from flat, dusty desert to a rockier terrain. Rocky outcrops littered the landscape, and in the distance, Elin could see the dark smudge of a mountain range.

She had to admit there was something stark and

imposing about the desert. Maybe because it made her feel so small. She might have to think about coming back here and going on safari. She gave a mental snort. Right, like she had time for a vacation.

"I'm glad we aren't covering this ground with wagons, like Farini did," Hale said.

"Absolutely." It would have been a hard, uncomfortable trek.

Hale stared toward the west. "You really think King Solomon hid something out here?"

Elin tried to imagine people mining in this unforgiving land and preparing shipments of ivory, gold, and diamonds to send north to a foreign king. "I think it is a likely location for Ophir. There is a good source of gold, diamonds, and ivory here. Solomon received shipments from Ophir every three years, so I doubt Ophir was close to Israel. Whether he sent some treasure back to be stored here, I don't know, but Claude and Silk Road believe it."

Claude lead them off the established track they'd been following. The Land Rover bumped over rough ground, and Elin gave up on reading her tablet. God, she felt like her bones were rattling. She gripped the handhold above her window.

"If there's a track here, I can't see it," Hale said. His large hands gripped the steering wheel tight as he maneuvered them over the rough ground.

"He must be following something from Farini's journal," she said.

They fell into silence as they continued northwest. She guessed they'd hit the Namibian border before too long.

"I did research on the Kalahari before the mission, and I read an interesting legend that's told in this area," Hale said. "About a place called the Bushman's Paradise."

"Oh?" She turned in her seat. "I haven't heard this one."

"There are variations of the tale, but it talks about a secret place in the desert where there is a freshwater spring, and kids play with diamonds as big as their fists."

He was getting into the spirit of the story, his tone deep and musical. The man could read her dry mission reports and make them sound good.

"There is one story that tells about a diary that was found, written by a survivor of a shipwreck. He was taken in by the San people, and taken to the Paradise. They killed him to protect its location."

Elin made a skeptical noise.

"Another story is about a German soldier who was taken to the Paradise by a local guide. He was amazed by the place, and took some diamonds. Years later, he went back, trying to find it again."

"And?" Despite herself, she found herself caught up in the tale.

Hale lowered his voice. "He was found dead in the desert, poison arrows in his back, and his pockets filled with diamonds."

"You believe every fantastic story you hear, Carter?"

He shot her one of those mega-watt smiles and her gaze dropped to his mouth. He had full, well-shaped lips.

"I've seen some pretty fantastic stuff at THS."

She nodded and jerked her gaze off his mouth. "Like lost oases in Egypt, mythical jewels in Asia, and South American jungle salves that can heal wounds in minutes?"

His smile widened. "That's right. It makes me wonder what other fantastic things are out there, buried and hidden away by time."

Ahead, she saw taillights come on and she straightened. "We're slowing down." She leaned forward, looking through the windshield. "Look."

A rocky outcrop rose up, covered in piles of large, blocky stones.

The vehicles pulled to a stop at the base of the hill. There were several large blocks of rock stacked in places, hardy shrubs growing in between.

It almost looked like the tumbled remains of a structure. The large blocks were regular-shaped and stacked. But the more she looked at it, the more it looked like a natural, evolutionary formation.

"Does that look like an outpost of an ancient lost city to you?" she asked.

Hale opened his door, letting the desert heat in. "No, but I never assume anything at first glance. Let's take a look around."

The rest of the team members were exiting their Land Rovers, and Elin did the same, jamming her hat on her head. The heat hit her in the face, and she carefully picked her way across the rocky ground.

Claude flung an arm out at the outcrop. "This is the location of the Ophir outpost that Farini discovered." The Silk Road leader's smile was wide, eagerness radiating off him. "Farini mentioned finding engravings carved into the rocks. That's where we should find the key leading to Ophir itself. Spread out. Find it!"

Side-by-side, Elin and Hale climbed the rocky hill. Hale pulled a little ahead of her, and instantly her gaze dropped down to where his cargo pants hugged his very fine ass. As he climbed, she watched the flex of muscles under the dark fabric.

Elin tripped on a rock and fell forward.

Shit. Before her face smashed into stone, a strong hand wrapped around her arm and broke her fall.

"Watch your step, Alex." A small smile flirted on his lips.

Busted. Elin huffed out a breath. This time, she kept her gaze firmly on the ground, and not her partner's ass.

They reached the top, and the air caught in Elin's lungs. She took a second to admire the desert vista spread out before her. The mountains were sharp peaks on the horizon, and the afternoon sun turned the sands a beautiful red-gold. For a second, she felt very small and insignificant.

"It's beautiful, isn't it?" he mused. "Even though it's deadly."

She looked at him, and saw he was watching her.

"I've always liked things that are more than they seem," he said. "Things that surprise me at every turn."

She raised a brow. "And things that could kill you if you aren't too careful?"

He looked like he was fighting a smile. "That just makes it more exciting."

"Are we talking about the desert, Carter?"

"You know what we're talking about."

She stepped up close to him, feeling the heat of him, and picking up the scent of healthy male sweat. "We are on a dangerous mission. That's the only thing we should be thinking about."

His lips twitched. "I wasn't the one who almost faceplanted into the rocks because I wasn't watching where I was going."

Insufferable man. "I'm going to do my job." She stomped over to a nearby pile of rocks. Putting Hale Carter out of her head, she circled the rocks, studying them. The blocks were mostly regular, but some weren't. She didn't see any chisel marks or engravings.

Hale came up beside her. "What do you think?" she asked.

He frowned, staring out across the rocky outcrop. "These look natural to me."

She pointed up to a higher point on the hill. "Let's take a look up there." She saw a larger rock balanced on a smaller rock. It looked precarious.

As they climbed up, she noticed sweat soaking

the collar of Hale's shirt, and she found herself staring at him again. *God, get a grip, Elin.* Clearly, she needed to start dating again as soon as she got back to DC. Or maybe she'd be in Europe with the Interpol team, and she could find some sexy guy with an accent.

They came to a stop. The base of the stack of rocks was large and rectangular. She climbed over them, standing in the center. Her pulse leaped as she looked out at the desert. She turned slowly, taking in the unimpeded view.

"It almost looks like this was a tower," Hale said. "The walls have all tumbled down, but this spot would have given them an excellent vantage point to spot anything coming this way."

She moved over to the rocks that might have formed the walls of the tower. She pressed her fingers to the stone and felt the day's heat in it. Then, small grooves caught her fingertips.

She peered more intently at the stone. The grooves were worn, and filled with crusted dirt. Crouching, she grabbed her water bottle off her belt and splashed some water on the rock. She felt Hale close behind her. He let out a whistle.

Her heart knocked against her chest. The markings were unmistakably engravings.

Chapter Six

Hale took in the faded, worn marks. It wasn't any language he recognized, but he knew it was old.

"Jesus," Elin whispered. "Carter, these symbols are Phoenician."

He frowned. "Phoenician?"

She nodded. "Solomon was allies with the Phoenicians and their king, Hiram." She looked up. "He hired the Phoenicians to build his temple. They were accomplished architects and builders. But more than that, they were expert seafarers. Their ships traveled all over the world."

"Solomon also hired them for their ships?"

"Yes. Many scholars believe that Solomon used Phoenician ships to transport goods from Ophir. There are even references to Hiram demanding more payment for his work on the temple and Solomon promising him a trip to Ophir."

"Can you read Phoenician?"

"No." She lifted her phone and snapped a picture. "And these engravings aren't complete."

"It looks like there was another rock on top of it." Hale looked around and then bent down, turning rocks over. Elin moved to help.

He turned a large rock over and went still. "Alex?"

She spun and gasped. "God, the engravings are pristine."

At some point, long ago, the rock had fallen facedown, which had protected the engravings. He stared at the scratch-like characters.

Elin carefully reached out and touched one, wonder on her face. Hale paused, his gaze zeroed in on her features. He'd never expected to see the no-nonsense FBI agent look at anything like that.

She snapped another picture. "You'd better call Claude over."

Hale moved to the other side of the hill. He yelled and waved his arms until the rest of their group headed in their direction.

Claude crested the hill and hurried up to the rocks, jubilant. "I knew we'd find it! Well done."

Sabine sauntered in after him, shooting Hale a look. He wasn't sure if the woman wanted to strip him naked or kill him. She was a hard one to read.

"What's it say?" Claude said to Rex.

Hale had learned that Rex was Claude's archeologist. The blond man knelt and studied the inscriptions.

"You know Phoenician?" Elin asked skeptically.

Rex nodded. "I know several ancient languages." The man moved his fingers over the markings.

As the minutes ticked by, Claude got more agitated. "Where do we go next? What does it say?"

"Patience. Some of these are quite worn." Rex looked up with a smile. "But there is a reference to

Ophir here. And a mountain of gold."

Behind Hale, he heard the excited rumbles from the rest of the team.

"Well, this could mean north..." Rex mused. "But it's not quite right."

"You need to work faster," Claude snapped. "We'll lose the light soon."

"Baby," Sabine drawled. "We've got this."

Claude swung around, muttering in French. He kicked some small rocks, sending them skittering down the side of the hill.

Hale glanced west, and saw that the sun would be setting soon. The desert was already changing color, the gold turning more red. They needed to set up camp before it got too late. It wasn't a good idea to be wandering around in the dark with wildlife out on the prowl.

"We need to set up camp," Hale said.

Claude's face twisted into a scowl. "Just take some pictures and keep working on it after we set up camp," he barked at Rex. "We'll camp here, in case you need to see these again in the morning."

The beleaguered archaeologist nodded, pulling out a large camera to take several high-resolution shots.

Soon, the group headed back down the hill toward their vehicles.

"Someone start a fire," Claude ordered. "We want to keep the wildlife away."

Everyone set to work. Hale and Elin grabbed their gear from their Land Rover. Nearby, Sabine was setting up a small, portable camp shower.

Several of the men were setting up camp chairs, angling them to face the magnificent sunset.

Elin climbed up on the back bumper of the Land Rover and started untying the cover on the rooftop tent packed on the roof. "Hope you don't snore."

Hale paused.

"Problem?" she asked.

"I'm…a restless sleeper."

"You should be too tired to toss and turn." She reached up and unfolded the tent. It was like opening a clam shell. A platform folded out over the side of the vehicle, with a ladder extending down to the ground. The khaki tent was attached to the platform.

"It's not that." God, how to tell her he hadn't slept beside a woman since he'd left the Navy?

Blue eyes met his and her expression softened. "What is it, Carter?"

"I have nightmares." He felt his muscles stiffening. "Sometimes I wake up and don't know where I am. I could hurt you."

She reached out, her fingers brushing his arm. "It's okay. I'm a trained agent and I'll make sure that doesn't happen."

He blew out a breath. No way he'd risk hurting her. He could foresee a long, sleepless night ahead.

They got their sleeping bags and other gear stored inside the tent. It was only just big enough for two, and Hale wasn't a small guy. It would be a tight fit.

Rex was sitting near his vehicle, hunched over his work, with a small lantern set up beside his chair. The rest of the Silk Road team was sitting around the fire—eating, drinking beers, and laughing. Hale and Elin sat by their Land Rover, quietly eating their meals.

Claude stood and took a long pull from his beer. "I'm going to be rich beyond my wildest dreams!" He lifted his bottle into the air. "*Santé.*"

Hale picked at his food, and Elin did the same beside him.

"This is a great first date," he said. "Firelight, great meal, good company."

Elin raised a brow. "I'd prefer a nice Shiraz, a steak—" she lowered her voice "—and no criminals."

"I'll remember that." He looked over, watching as night crept over the desert and a mass of stars blinked to life overhead.

"Hey, Carter," one of the Silk Road guys called out. "You're ex-military, right?"

"Yeah," he replied, turning his head.

"What was your worst mission? We're trading war stories."

Hale stiffened, ugly memories trying to break free. His chest felt tight. "They were all bad."

He turned his back to the group and he heard a few grumbles, but soon they forgot about him and kept talking among themselves.

Elin was watching him.

"Your last mission was bad," she said quietly. "The one that caused you to quit the SEALs."

Hale ground his teeth together, well aware that her words were statements, not questions. "You read my file. I don't talk about it. It's done. Gone."

"Does ignoring it work?"

Now he looked at her, anger thrumming through his veins. "You going to tell me I need to talk it out? Go to therapy? Relive every fucking thing that happened? Maybe I should do some yoga and meditation while I'm at it?"

"Yes. Talking about it could help. I've had assignments go bad—"

He jerked to his feet. "Have you been tortured? Had your fingers broken one by one? Have you failed your friends and watched them get tortured and killed?"

She bit her lip. "No."

"So don't pretend you can understand what I need. Like I said, I don't talk about it. Let's just focus on the mission."

"Hale—"

Suddenly, heated voices broke out around the fire. They both turned. Claude was squaring off with Rex, berating the archaeologist.

"You should have the direction by now!" Claude yelled. "Where is Ophir?"

"I need some more time—"

"Sucks to be Rex." Hale dropped back into his chair.

"Claude is impatient." Elin pulled up her own image on her phone in her lap. "I looked up some Phoenician and I think we do need to go north. It's the distance that's problematic. It references an *ell*." She pulled a face. "It was a biblical unit of measurement, but the Phoenician *ell* was slightly different to a standard *ell* and there is also the Hebrew *cubit* to consider."

Suddenly, there were startled shouts, and Claude pulled a pistol from his waistband. He aimed it at the archaeologist and fired.

Rex flew backward, landing among the rocks, not moving.

Elin shot to her feet and Hale grabbed her arm to keep her from moving forward. Everyone was silent.

"He was holding us up on purpose." Claude's face was eerily composed. "He was the Treasure Hunter Security spy!"

"Sweetie, you need to chill," Sabine drawled. She held up a beer. "If you kill all of our team, we'll never reach Ophir."

Everyone watched in tense silence, waiting to see what Claude would do next.

Hale kept his fingers flexed, ready to reach for his SIG tucked at his hip. But then the tension drained from the Frenchman. He took the beer from Sabine and tipped the bottle back, taking a long drink. Then dropped down into a chair.

Suddenly, Elin strode toward Claude. Cursing, Hale hurried to keep up with her.

"I took a good look at the engravings," she said. "I think I know the way." She shot Rex's body a single glance before looking back at Claude.

Hale knew the man's death had to affect her. She was an FBI agent, and she was good at it. But she was putting it aside to stay on track with the mission.

"We definitely have to head north," she said. "My best guess, we need to travel about two hundred kilometers to get there. My calculation of ancient distance units might be a bit off, though."

"*Merci*, Alex," Claude said. "Finally, some competence." He leaned back in his chair. "Westcott, you are on watch. Thompson, take Van Wyk to help you bury Rex's body. We don't need it here in camp luring the wildlife. Everybody, relax and get some rest. We leave at first light."

Elin and Hale headed toward their vehicle. "You get ready first," Hale said. "Let me grab a few things, and I'll take a shower."

He felt tension spike between them. As he grabbed some fresh clothes, Elin climbed up the ladder to the tent.

Hale headed for the shower, keen to splash some water over his head. Some cold water might help the fact that despite everything going on, his body was excruciatingly aware that he was going to spend the night with Elin Alexander. He headed toward the camp shower and pulled up short.

Sabine slipped out from behind the sheet of canvas someone had rigged around the shower. She was naked. She smiled at him, running her towel over her wet hair.

"Planning to take a shower?" she asked.

"Uh, no." Not anymore. He gave her a wide berth and reached for the water container. He tipped some out and washed his face.

Sabine moved up behind him, her body brushing against his. She smelled strongly of coconut.

"I'd love to see you naked. Is it true that black men have big cocks?"

Charming. "I'm only half African American, so I'm probably not a good test case."

Her hand touched his ass. "I bet yours is mighty fine, Carter. I'd love to have a play."

He straightened and stepped away. "I'm tired and headed to bed."

Her face twisted unattractively. "With your pretty blonde. She doesn't seem your type."

Like she knew him or his type. "Good night."

He didn't hurry back to his tent, but damn, he wanted to. He climbed up the ladder and into the tent. Inside, Elin was lying on her side on her sleeping bag, just covered by a light sheet. A compact electric lantern glowed beside her. She was tapping notes into her tablet.

She raised a brow. "Thought you were taking a shower."

"Change of plans. I'll just wash up and change here."

"Why do you smell like Sabine?"

He shifted to dig through his bag for his wet wipes. "Let's just say she made me an offer I was happy to refuse...and forgo my shower."

Elin made a sound and clicked the lantern off. Hale quickly wiped himself over and changed his clothes for fresh ones. Since it was hot, he left his shirt off.

After his eyes adjusted, he could tell she was lying flat on her back. He lay down on his sleeping bag, excruciatingly conscious that they were almost hip to hip, and only inches away from each other.

The tension was thick.

Shit, if he fell asleep and had a nightmare, he really could hurt her.

"I'm not sure sharing a tent is a good idea." Her voice broke the darkness.

He tried to keep things light. "Don't think you can control yourself?"

She made a scoffing sound. "Nothing wrong with your ego, is there?" She was silent for a second. "Claude killed Rex like he was nothing. No hesitation, no thought, no remorse." Her voice had lowered to a soundless whisper, conscious of not being overheard.

"He'll kill anyone who gets in his way," Hale said.

"I know."

Her voice sounded odd, and he tried to see more of her in the darkness. "Elin? What is it?"

"Silk Road killed my father."

"What?" He sat up. "When?"

"I was thirteen."

"Hell."

"They were barely getting started back then. My mother restores art, primarily paintings. They broke into our home to steal the painting she was working on. My father tried to stop them."

"I'm sorry."

"They took the painting, and for several horrible weeks, my mother was the main suspect." A harsh expulsion of air. "It tarnished her career, even after she was exonerated. I won't let them keep doing it."

"That's why you joined the FBI?"

"No. I wanted to be a police officer from the time I started school. But once I learned about the Art Crime Team, yes, Silk Road was a big factor for me joining. I've been working my butt off to bring them down, and if I pull this mission off, there's a promotion waiting for me."

"Sounds important."

"It is. I'd join an Interpol task force and have a greater reach to keep fighting Silk Road and other antiquities thieves. Plus, I'd get to live in France. I've always wanted to stand on top of the Eiffel Tower and know I've achieved what I worked for." Her voice lowered. "And know that Silk Road can't destroy some other kid's life."

"I have your back." Hale reached out and took her hand, squeezing it. "I won't let any of these people hurt you."

"I can protect myself, Carter, and I won't let any of them hurt you, either."

He blinked. He was a protector. Hell, he'd made a career out of it. When had anyone ever said they'd protect him? "I'm sorry about your dad, and what happened to your mom."

"Thanks." She cleared her throat. "Now, say something arrogant again, instead of being a good guy."

He rolled over, looking at the pale oval of her face in the darkness. "I am a good guy."

Pulled by something he didn't quite understand, he moved closer. She didn't move away, and he sensed her gaze on him.

"Except when I'm bad. Because with the right woman, one who is extremely sexy doing her job, one with a sharp mind that I love to watch at work, and one with tightly-toned curves and an ass I'm begging to hold in my hands, and a mouth I want to taste—"

"I think you made your point." Her voice was husky.

"Then I can be very bad," he murmured.

He heard her breath hitch. "We have a mission, a—"

"Dangerous one. I know. That's why I haven't touched you, and I won't." He made a strangled sound. "And why I have to try and get some rest with a painful hard-on."

Elin was silent. Suddenly, she sat up and faced him. He could just make out her bare shoulders and the thin straps of her tank top.

Then, she leaned over and kissed him, sending shock rocketing through his body. It was a light kiss. A testing taste, rather than a full kiss.

She pulled back, and they stared at each other.

Damn, she tasted so good. Hale wrapped his arms around her and yanked her closer. Her hands gripped his shoulders, and she slithered into his lap. Her mouth opened and Hale took.

Their tongues twined, and he felt heat explode through him, his cock throbbing. She kissed him like she needed him more than air, and he fucking loved it. Elin Alexander was wild under her FBI gloss.

She yanked back, panting. They stared at each

other in the darkness.

He gripped her hips. "Elin—"

She shook her head. "Ah…that got a bit out of control."

And something told him Elin didn't like losing control.

She scooted back onto her sleeping bag. Arousal still sang through Hale's blood, and he flexed his hands on his sleeping bag. He wanted more. He wanted to touch and taste every part of her. He wanted her laid out naked before him, ready for his fingers, his mouth, his cock.

A breath shuddered out of him. Sex was fun. He liked the hell out of it. But it didn't usually leave him feeling this jittery and on edge.

"I think we need to cool it off," Elin said. "And remember our mission."

Frustration bit at him. She was in full retreat. "You want to pretend it didn't happen?"

"I don't pretend anything, Carter. It happened. Now we move on." She yanked her sheet up.

He laughed. "Right. You keep telling yourself that, Elin."

"What's that mean?"

He reached out and ran his thumb over her lips. She went still, but he felt her lips part.

Oh, yeah. She wanted him. "You know what that means." Then he pulled back, lay down, and rolled over.

He heard her plump her pillow and lie down, too. Fuck, his skin was still hot. He wanted to reach for her and pull her under him until she was begging him to touch her.

He listened to her toss and turn, and her obvious discomfort made him smile. Good.

Then he stared at the wall of the tent and wondered how the hell *he* was going to make it through the night.

Chapter Seven

When Elin woke, she found her face pressed against a hard, firm chest. She breathed deep, snuggling in. He was warm and he smelled good.

He smelled like Hale.

Hale.

She jerked back and sat up. He was awake, and looking at her with a sexy, sleepy smile. "Why aren't you asleep?" It was still dark and she guessed dawn was still several hours away.

"I told you I wouldn't risk hurting you in my sleep."

He'd stayed awake. To protect her. Something inside her softened. "You need to rest, Hale. I told you, I can handle it."

He shook his head.

"Look, I've had several hours' sleep. You rest now, and I'll keep watch."

He looked uncertain.

"I need you in top form, Carter, not falling asleep."

He gave a reluctant nod. "Okay, but if I have a nightmare—"

"I'll wake you."

He slid an arm under his head and in the darkness, she could just make out a shadow of a tattoo on his shoulder.

"So, how do you sleep with your girlfriends?" Elin rolled her eyes and wished she'd bitten her tongue.

"I don't have girlfriends. And I...ah, never stay the night. I wouldn't risk it, even if I wanted to."

Oh. Elin lay in the darkness, listening as his breathing evened out and his body relaxed. She promised herself that he'd get a few decent hours of sleep.

The murky light of dawn was filling the tent when she next opened her eyes. Shit, she'd fallen asleep. And somehow, she was wrapped tightly in Hale's arms, her face pressed to his hard chest again.

Her gaze traced over hard pecs. His right shoulder and muscled arm were inked with a fascinating black swirl of a tattoo. His face was relaxed, his breathing even. Looked like he'd slept just fine.

Desire was a hot curl in her belly. God, what the hell was she doing? She pulled away from him.

His arms tightened. "Elin?"

"I'll go and wash up."

He released her and rolled over. She grabbed her backpack and ducked out of the tent. She wasn't running. She wasn't afraid.

She headed toward the shower. A few of the others were already up and making coffee on the fire. She stepped inside the shower canvas and quickly stripped off. Then she scraped a hand over her face. Oh, God, she was in trouble.

She stepped under the lukewarm water. The cool morning air made her nipples tighten, and her churning thoughts turned to Hale. Damn the man. She pressed her hand to her belly. She really, really wanted to slide her hand lower and touch herself.

But then someone near the campfire coughed and she shook her head. She flicked off the water, toweled off, and pulled on fresh clothes. She took a deep breath and headed out.

Hale had already packed up the tent, and was loading their things in their Land Rover. He handed her a plate. "Breakfast."

She eyed the bread and eggs. "Thanks."

"Alex—"

She smiled brightly. "We have a big day ahead."

"I thought we weren't pretending?"

"I'm not." God, now she was a liar, as well.

He leaned closer. "I just wanted to thank you."

"For what?"

"For the best sleep I've had in a long time." He stalked away to finish packing up the last of their gear, and left her staring at him.

When Claude called for them to move out, she strode over to the driver's seat. "I'm driving today."

"All yours," Hale said.

Soon, the convoy pulled out. Elin focused on the rough ground, driving slowly and carefully. The minutes blurred as they headed north, the monotony of the desert landscape a lulling backdrop.

Minutes turned to hours. She and Hale speculated more on King Solomon and the mysterious treasure. They ate some biltong—South African jerky—and trail mix.

Elin eventually decided she wasn't coming back here on safari. In fact, she was pretty sure she'd be avoiding deserts for a while.

"There," Hale called out.

Elin straightened, and spotted another rocky outcrop in the distance. This one rose up sharply from the flat land around it.

The other vehicles veered off course, and Elin followed. As they got closer, she sucked in a breath. "Hale."

"I see it."

A circular structure was built on top of the hill. "This one is definitely man-made."

***

Hale carefully climbed up the rocks. They passed under an imposing stone archway, still standing after all this time. He saw a small lizard dart away.

Amazing. There was no doubt that this was an ancient structure.

As they neared the peak, he studied the stone-built formation. It was incredible, but it didn't look like a sprawling city.

"This isn't Ophir," Sabine said.

Claude frowned. "No."

"It must be another outpost," Elin said.

Claude flipped from despondent to excited, looking around eagerly. "Fan out. There must be more engravings."

Elin moved up beside Hale, and they climbed up to the structure. They skirted around the circular wall.

"Claude reminds me of a bomb about to go off," Hale murmured quietly.

Elin nodded. "Let's hope we find something, and quick." Her face sharpened and she leaned closer to Hale, her voice a murmur. "Then we let him lead us to Ophir, find out what treasure he's looking for, and then we call in our team and take them all down."

Hale stepped into the structure and held out a hand to Elin. She put her hand in his, and they walked into the center.

Part of the wall had tumbled down long ago, but the rest of it was still intact. Hale moved forward, trying to imagine the people who'd stood here before him. The people of Ophir.

"Imagine what this looked like back in its heyday." He turned, looking across the hill. There were more tumbled rocks. The structure would have been substantial.

Elin looked out across the desert. "I can see huge convoys loaded with gold, diamonds, and ivory heading to the sea. It must've been incredible."

"Getting fanciful, Alex?"

She pulled a face at him.

Once again, Hale felt that hit of heat to his gut.

He liked lots of things about Elin Alexander. Hell, he liked the entire sexy, competent package, and wanted to see more of it.

"Who were the people of Ophir?" he asked.

"I don't know. The local San people have been here a long time, but they're semi-nomadic, and descended from hunter-gatherers."

"Who didn't build vast rock-cut cities."

"Right. But they talked of an Old Race. So, maybe some of their ancestors or a neighboring race?"

Suddenly, he heard a noise. A buzzing sound. He tilted his head, looking up into the blue sky.

Elin frowned, turning around slowly, her ponytail swinging out behind her. "What's that?"

Hale had done enough work with them to know. "A drone."

The small aircraft rounded the rock wall, rising up above them. It was black and, from the look of it, military grade. It was also equipped with weapons.

Hale watched as the two guns swiveled in his and Elin's direction.

Fuck. He dived, tackling Elin to the ground. She grunted, and they slid toward the edge of the rock platform.

Gunfire sprayed the rock all around them. *Fuck, fuck, fuck.*

"Up." He grabbed Elin's arm and yanked her to her feet. Together, they scrambled over the edge.

They both slipped on small rocks as they slid down the hill. More gunfire hit, frighteningly close by, and Hale yanked Elin behind another rock wall.

"Keep moving."

Ducking down, they kept running over the rough ground. Then, he heard the buzzing sound again. The drone reappeared in front of them, coming out from behind a tower of rocks.

"This way!" Elin yanked Hale in a different direction. Together, they dove inside another semi-circular structure.

Gunfire roared around them. Rock chips hit Hale's face, stinging. He swiped at his forehead, and his hand came away streaked with blood.

Beside him, Elin yanked out her Glock, and Hale did the same with his SIG.

"It has us pinned down." She popped up, aiming over the rock wall. She took a shot.

Bullets peppered the wall around them, and she ducked back down. Hale waited, and when the firing stopped, he rose and fired.

"Can you distract it?" Elin asked. "If you can get it facing in a different direction, I'll have a better shot at it."

"You sure you can hit it?" he asked.

More gunfire, which caused them both to hunker down. "Yes."

He had no doubt. He'd seen her at the firing range, and besides, Elin would never embellish her skills. He nodded, took a deep breath, and moved toward the edge of the rock wall.

"Hale." She grabbed his shoulder.

He turned his head and realized her face was right there, a heartbeat from his.

She pressed a quick, fleeting kiss to his lips. "Be careful."

He gave her a nod, and then spun around the wall. He leaped up and sprinted. A spray of gunfire hit the ground, and he dived and rolled, ignoring the rocks biting into his body.

He jumped back to his feet, dodging around some larger rocks. Suddenly, the drone sliced to the right in a fast move, cutting in front of him. It swiveled to face him.

Fuck. He slid in behind a small boulder. It was barely big enough to cover him. He ducked down, and gunfire peppered around him.

"Come on, Elin," he muttered.

He heard her Glock firing. The sound of the drone changed, but then, more gunfire hit right near him.

He looked back behind him and saw the rest of their group rushing toward them. Claude was yelling.

Bang. Bang. Bang.

Elin was firing again. Suddenly, the drone gunfire stopped. Hale looked around the edge of the rock.

The drone was smoking and drunkenly flying sideways. He looked over, and saw Elin standing on a rock wall. She had her gun aimed at the drone, and with blue sky behind her, she was a clear target.

He saw the wobbling drone turn, and its guns swiveled toward Elin.

Without thinking, Hale leaped up, sprinting

toward her, his arms pumping. He expected to see bullets hit her body at any minute.

He wasn't going to fucking watch her die. He reached her, and even though she was still firing at the drone, he snatched her off the wall.

"Hale!"

"You're a fucking perfect target."

"I needed a good shot." She turned in his arms. "Look."

The drone was flying off, wobbling from side to side. Together, they watched it career out over the desert, and a second later, it crashed into the sand.

**

Elin slipped her Glock back into her holster. Behind her, she heard Hale drag in a deep breath. She looked at him and froze. He was covered in blood.

What the hell? "Were you hit?" She patted his chest, looking at the spots of blood, her heart racing. "Did it get you?"

They were in the middle of nowhere. If he was badly hurt—

He grabbed her wrists. "Elin. I'm fine. I just got hit by rock chips."

She tried to calm her pulse. His handsome face was covered in small nicks, and there was a bad one on the side of his neck, blood sliding down into his shirt.

The panic drained out of her. They'd been shot at and nearly killed, but they were alive.

"I'm still pissed at you," he ground out. "Standing on top of that wall like a fucking superhero."

She ignored him, leaped up, and wrapped her legs around his waist. He reacted instantly, his hands sliding under her ass, and then she didn't know if it was her kissing him, or him kissing her. All she knew was that he had the best lips—full and firm—and the man was a mighty fine kisser. As his tongue tangled with hers, she felt the shock of sensation right down to her bones.

He paused to tease her lips, his hands clenching on her buttocks. Then, he dived deep again, and every one of Elin's thoughts were centered on Hale, and how much she wanted him.

His mouth moved along her jaw, teeth nipping at sensitive skin. "First second I laid eyes on you, I knew."

"I know." She'd felt it, too.

Dimly, she heard shouts, and the sound of the others getting closer. Hale took her mouth one last time—hard and insistent—like he needed one last taste to survive. She reluctantly pulled back, and Hale stared at her with unreadable eyes.

"Whoa," she murmured. "Well, that was..."

"Whoa works for me."

The first of the group crested the hill, and Hale let Elin's legs drop back to the ground. Claude appeared, incandescent with rage.

"What the hell was that?" He tossed his hands in the air. He started ranting in French, before he switched back to English. "They want the ring. It's *my* ring, *my* treasure."

Elin eyed the Frenchman as he started pacing with jerky steps. So it was a ring. Any piece of jewelry that could be linked to King Solomon would be highly valuable. But if this was about *the* Seal of Solomon...well, that was something different.

"I very much doubt the FBI or THS would send a drone to mow us down," Elin said. "So, who the hell are these other players you mentioned?"

"I don't know. But I won't rule out this drone belonging to the FBI or THS." Claude's eyes flashed. "This treasure is enough to make people do desperate things."

A cold shiver skated down Elin's spine, despite the heat. If it was that valuable, how far would Claude go? And more than that, what would he do if he discovered who Elin and Hale really were?

"Boss, we found the inscription," the woman, Thompson, called out.

Anger over the drone attack was replaced by excitement over the new engravings. Elin fell into step with Hale, as they crossed the hill to another ruined structure. Sabine was crouched down by the end of the circular rock wall, and Elin spotted the markings etched into the stone.

"Alex?" Claude waved at the rocks.

"I'm not an expert, Claude. So don't shoot the messenger if I can't translate this." Sabine moved aside, and Elin crouched down. Hale towered over her and she looked up. He crossed his arms over his chest, menacing and protective. She felt a glow of warmth in her chest.

Elin pulled her small backpack off and prayed her tablet hadn't been damaged in the wild rush to escape the drone. She slid it out, and it was fine, thanks to its heavy-duty case. She focused on the symbols and got to work. She tapped in her translation, changing a few things, and taking her time on some of the harder symbols.

"We aren't far," she said. "It talks about reaching a mountain. We need to head west until we find the mountain."

Hale held out a hand for her tablet and she handed it over. He tapped and when she peered over, she saw he'd pulled up satellite maps of the area.

He frowned. "There are no mountains west of our location." He spun it around so she could see the flat terrain.

"Damn. Let me check my translation again." She ran over the inscriptions once more, and heaved out a breath. "It definitely says a mountain, and definitely west of here."

"It has to be there," Claude said. "We go west and follow the instructions." He scanned the sky. "And we travel fast. Whoever the hell sent the drone isn't going to give up. If we travel quickly, we might reach the mines before dark."

They climbed back down the hill. Back at the Land Rover, Elin was happy to let Hale drive. She fastened her seatbelt, and they pulled out behind the others.

"Some of those cuts look bad," she said.

Hale swiped his sleeve over his face. "They're

fine. I'll deal with them later." He glanced her way. "If we find the mine, we call in Dec."

She nodded. "If we find it, it'll be time to really ruin Claude's week." She glanced ahead. "Who was controlling the drone?"

"I don't know. Maybe Silk Road has a rival."

They kept driving through the heat of the day. Soon, the noon heat gave way to the afternoon. Off in the distance, she saw the silhouettes of some animals, but they were too far away to tell what they were.

As the sun sank toward the horizon, there was no sign of a mountain or any ancient mines. Finally, Claude pulled over. One look at the man's face said he wasn't happy.

They all set up camp, and this time, there was no fireside revelry. Instead, the group was tense and unhappy.

Elin climbed into her and Hale's tent and flicked on the lantern. Hale came in behind her. She eyed the dried blood on his scratches. The one on his neck was still bleeding dully.

"Let me clean those scratches." She fished around for her first aid kit.

"I told you they're okay." He sat down and winced. "I think I have a couple on my chest as well."

"Stop being a baby and let me sort them out."

He grabbed the back of his stained shirt and yanked it over his head.

Holy hell. Elin stared at all the solid muscles. She hadn't really gotten a full, unimpeded view of him that morning. The guy clearly spent all his time working out.

His shoulders were broad and toned, his arms were unreal. She slid her gaze down his chest, taking in the small cuts across his pecs, before she looked down at the tight ridges of his stomach.

"Don't think I have any scratches down there," Hale said in a dry voice.

She jerked her gaze up. "Sorry, I was just taking it all in. You are in excellent shape."

His teeth flashed. "Thanks."

Forcing herself to focus, Elin pulled some antiseptic wipes out of the first aid kit. She moved closer, and started cleaning the cuts on his chest.

Every now and then, her fingers brushed his skin. He felt so hard and so hot. Her breathing sped up, and a damp ache started between her legs.

She grabbed a clean wipe and started on the cuts on his face.

"I want you naked, Elin." His voice was deep and gruff.

She stilled, her gaze locking with his. She saw need burning there, and she wasn't sure anyone had ever wanted her as much as Hale did.

"I want to mess up that neat, efficient tidiness you have. Even in the middle of the desert, you look put-together."

Her breath caught in her throat, and need was a hard, vicious thing.

"Are you turned on?" he murmured.

"Yes." Her hand was a little shaky as she swiped at the last cut on his neck.

He lifted a hand, his thumb stroking across her lips. "I want to kiss you, taste you, watch your face as I slide inside you."

His deep voice scraped over her enflamed nerves. "I want that, too." She nipped the end of his thumb and saw his chest shudder. "I want to see every inch of your incredible body. I want you on top of me, under me, inside me."

Hale let out a ragged breath. "Not tonight." His voice was a growl. "I need time to make love to you properly, and I need to keep you safe. It sure as hell won't be while we are surrounded by fucking Silk Road, and with an unknown assailant sending drones after us."

It made sense, but her needy body didn't like it.

"Soon," he said.

She nodded. "We'll see, Carter."

He shot her one of his bone-melting smiles. "You aren't going to make it easy, are you?"

"I think you've had enough easy." She flicked off the light. "I want you to sleep tonight."

He went still. "I'm not sure—"

"You slept this morning."

"I think...knowing you can handle yourself helped. And..."

She waited. "And?"

"Can I hold you?"

She trembled. "Yes."

They both lay down, but this time, he curled his big body around her, and she let him. She heard him let out a shuddering breath before he nuzzled his face into her hair.

Something felt far too right about relaxing into Hale Carter and drifting off to sleep.

Chapter Eight

Hale woke with his arms full of Elin. He lay there, just enjoying the simple act of holding her. Once again, he'd slept like a rock. No nightmares. No waking mid-scream. Holding her was something he could get used to.

He stilled, looking at the plastic of the tent. He'd never, ever wanted to get used to holding one particular woman before.

Slowly, the sounds of the others waking outside in the camp filtered through the nylon, and he felt Elin stir. When she stiffened, he knew she was awake.

"Are you going to run again?" he murmured.

"No." Her voice was husky with sleep.

Neither of them moved, holding each other as the colors of the breaking dawn lit the sky outside. He breathed in, pulling in the scent of her hair. She smelled like fresh water, even in the middle of the desert.

Suddenly, another sound broke the early morning stillness. A steady *thwap thwap thwap* in the distance.

Both he and Elin scrambled up, yanking on their clothes.

"Another drone?" she asked, pulling her hair back and tying it.

"No. Helicopter."

Dressed, they finished stuffing their gear into their bags, and climbed out of their tent. Outside, the rest of the group had gathered, looking toward the west. Hale threw their backpacks in their Land Rover, eyeing the incoming helicopter.

Had Dec decided to come in early?

Together, he and Elin closed up the rooftop tent and latched it down. Then they joined the group.

"Who is it?" Elin asked.

Claude had his hands on his hips, staring up at the chopper. When he turned to look at them, he had a sour look on his face. "It's my boss. He's one of Silk Road's top people."

Hale felt a rush through his veins. Dec had been trying to identify the group's top people for years. But as the chopper got closer, Hale's gut cramped.

Why was this guy coming in now? This couldn't be good. He moved closer to Elin.

The helicopter—a sleek black Airbus Colibri—landed just outside the camp, kicking up a swirl of dust. The door opened and a man, dressed in khaki outdoor gear, tossed a headset onto the seat and leaped out with athletic grace. He strode toward them, mirrored sunglasses hiding his eyes.

Hale finally got a good look at the man's face. "What the fuck?" he muttered under his breath.

Beside him, Elin shook her head, her face incredulous.

It was a very-well-known Hollywood actor. A

man famous for his action movies. Several tall, muscled, and armed men jumped out of the helicopter behind the man.

John Drift, million-dollar star, strode forward. He was far shorter than Hale had expected. "Claude. Update."

"We have the direction of Ophir and the mines."

The actor stopped. "But you haven't located the mine yet."

"We've found two outposts, each with engravings pointing to Ophir. The final engraving gave us the location of the mine."

"You have a problem," Drift said.

The man was so still. Hale watched him steadily. Like a damn tiger waiting to pounce.

"The drone," Claude said. "I know."

Drift froze. "Drone?"

Claude straightened. "Yes, we were attacked by an armed drone yesterday evening."

Drift cursed. "No, that's another issue to deal with. The problem I'm referring to is that I've learned you have an FBI agent and a Treasure Hunter Security agent undercover on your team."

All sound died away. Even the air was still.

Shit. Hale stayed calm and relaxed, ready for anything. He saw Elin doing the same, a perplexed frown furrowing her brow. Like this was all news to her.

"I took care of Rex," Claude said. "He was the undercover agent, and he was delaying our expedition."

Drift pulled his glasses off, his cold, blue gaze

sweeping over the group. His eyes touched Hale for just a second, but it was enough to know that he was dangerous. This was no simple actor.

"No." Drift turned back to Claude. "I think you're incompetent."

Claude spluttered, rounding to face the man. In a fast, experienced move, Drift yanked a pistol from a holster at his side. He aimed and shot Claude point-blank in the forehead.

A surprised look crossed Claude's face as he fell forward and collapsed on the ground.

Hale expected Sabine to explode into action to avenge her lover, but instead, she looked at Claude dispassionately. Then, she sauntered over to stand beside Drift and his guards.

The man turned toward Hale and Elin. He nodded, and his four guards moved forward. Hale and Elin found themselves flanked by the men. Two of them grabbed Hale's arms in a firm grip, taking his SIG.

"Hey, hands off," Elin snapped, yanking against her captors as they grabbed her. One man patted her down, taking her Glock and her tablet.

"Now, I want to know exactly what the FBI and Treasure Hunter Security know about our mission, Special Agent Alexander and Mr. Carter." Drift stared at them.

The others in their group gasped and cursed, staring at them.

"What is your plan?" Drift stepped closer, his gun still in his hand by his side. "I will not let anything jeopardize this mission, and I have no qualms about leaving your dead bodies here beside Claude's to rot in the desert sun."

***

Elin's heart was pounding. She was jerked roughly and patted down again.

"I'm a freelancer," she said. "I don't—"

The blow slammed into her cheek, knocking her sideways. She managed to keep her balance, and through the ringing in her head, she looked up. Beside her, Hale jerked against the men holding him, almost knocking them over.

She caught his eye and gave a quick shake of her head.

"I want the truth," Drift bit out.

Elin's mind whirled, trying to find a way out that kept her and Hale alive. "How did you find out?"

"I have *friends* in South African law enforcement. I got wind that one of our men in Cape Town had been brought in with FBI and THS assistance. I did some digging, and paid some bribes."

Dammit.

Drift nodded his head and one of the guards moved, knocked the butt of his assault rifle into the back of Hale's legs. He fell to his knees on the sand, glaring at Drift.

Then, a second guard stepped up behind Hale and drew a machete off his belt.

Elin's chest contracted.

"I'll have them start with Mr. Carter's hands, Agent Alexander."

"Fuck you," Hale said.

"You Navy SEALs are all just expendable grunts," Drift said.

Hale snorted. "Right, because being an actor is so intellectual."

"It's art. The world sees what I want them to see."

Elin took a step forward. If Hale kept taunting the man, he'd end up hacked to pieces. "The plan is to call for backup when we reach the mines. They'll come in from Namibia and arrest everyone."

Drift tilted his head. "How do you contact them?"

"My tablet," she lied.

One of the guards held it out, then threw it on the ground. The man brought his huge boot down on the device, smashing it to bits.

"What's so special about the mines?" Hale demanded. "Even if you find them, you can't exploit them. The government will discover you and shut you down."

"It's not about the mines," Drift answered.

"Right," Elin said. "It's about King Solomon's ring."

The man's blue eyes narrowed. "Claude had a big mouth." Then the actor shrugged one shoulder. "You'll be dead shortly, so I guess you deserve to know what you're dying for."

Elin turned her head enough to catch Hale's gaze. She nodded imperceptibly at their Land Rover and tried to communicate her plan to him.

She hoped to hell he understood.

He gave no reaction.

"The Seal of Solomon," Drift said. "That's what this is all about."

Elin's eyebrow shot up. "A ring that can control genies? You don't really believe that, do you?"

"Stories get twisted over time, Agent Alexander. All the stories that reference the Seal of Solomon talk of djinn, instantaneous travel, communication with animals, information on building great structures, and ways to gather immense wealth. The ring has a jewel on it, and I believe it is an uncut diamond."

Elin still wasn't sure how this made the ring worth all this trouble and death.

Drift moved closer, his square-jawed face animated. "I believe the ring is a repository of knowledge of an advanced race that flourished before devastating floods at the end of the last Ice Age destroyed their civilization."

Elin shook her head. "There is no proof that any advanced civilizations existed before the Ice Age floods."

A sharp smile. "You're wrong, Agent Alexander, and I will hold that proof in my hands. But I'm sorry to say that you and your friend Mr. Carter will not."

The man nodded at the guards.

"Hale, now!" Elin shouted.

In unison, both she and Hale exploded into action. She slammed her fist into the guard closest to her and spun to grab the second man. Out of the corner of her eye, she saw Hale fighting with his guards, landing brutal blows.

She heard Drift shouting as she grabbed the guard's shirt. She yanked him around, she slid her hand around the butt of his handgun, and pulled it out of the holster. Then she slammed him into Drift. Both men tumbled to the sand.

Elin ran for the Land Rover.

***

Hale landed a vicious kick on the man closest to him. The man fumbled for his gun, but Hale rammed a hard punch to the man's face. He groaned and went down.

Behind him, Hale saw one of the other guards bringing up a rifle.

Hale moved fast, grabbing the end of the rifle and yanking. The man got close enough, and Hale jabbed a hard chop to the man's throat. As he choked, Hale swung him around, using him as a shield.

Bullets slammed into the man, his body jerking.

Hale moved backward toward the Land Rover. He prayed no one aimed for Elin as she streaked toward the vehicle.

As his captive became deadweight, Hale shoved him toward the guard firing. Then he turned and ran. He caught up to Elin and grabbed her arm.

More gunfire ripped through the air. Hale yanked Elin down, and together they hit the ground.

"Stay low." They scrambled across the last few feet of sand and reached their vehicle.

Elin had managed to snatch a handgun from one of the guards. She swiveled on one knee and aimed behind them.

Hale closed the distance to the Land Rover. He wrenched open the passenger door, and dived across the vehicle for the driver's seat.

He started the engine, gunning it. Elin leaped into the car and slammed the door closed. Hale jammed the Land Rover into drive and slammed his foot down on the accelerator.

The back end of the vehicle skidded out behind them and Hale tightened his grip on the wheel, righting their wild slide. Bullets pinged off metal, and a window shattered.

"Down!" he shouted.

They bounced out onto the rough dirt track and sped off.

Staying low, Elin looked back behind them. "They're following. Two vehicles."

He sped up. "Put your belt on."

They both buckled in and Hale drove as fast as he could on the dirt road. If he rolled them, they were dead.

"They aren't following in the helicopter?" He tried to see anything through the dust cloud behind them.

"No. But the two Land Rovers are closing in fast."

Hale saw them now. The two pursuing vehicles moved up close behind them. One Land Rover jerked to the right, trying to come up beside them. Hale yanked the wheel, cutting him off.

"Hold on," he said grimly.

Elin glanced at him. "What are you—?"

He slammed on the brakes. They skidded to a halt and the Land Rover behind them rammed into the back of them.

They both pitched forward, but Hale was already pressing his foot back to the accelerator. They took off again.

"One down, one to go."

"You nearly killed us." Her tone was calm. "But good move."

He looked at her. Her face was set and focused. Nerves of steel.

Hale saw the second Land Rover appear out of the dust behind them. They weren't giving up.

The Land Rover put on a burst of speed and shot up close beside them. Hale looked over and saw the passenger window lowering. A rifle appeared, aiming at them.

Fuck. Hale jerked the wheel, ramming into the side of the other Land Rover.

He heard Elin curse, and the Silk Road Land Rover bounced off the track, onto rough ground, and rolled.

"Two down." He grinned.

She looked back behind them. "Sorry, but the first one is still coming."

In the rearview mirror, Hale saw the first Land Rover pulling up behind them. The front end was badly crumpled, but clearly still operational. *Dammit.*

Suddenly, gunshots shattered the window behind them. They both ducked.

Shit. If they lost their vehicle, they'd be as good as dead. They couldn't survive on foot in the Kalahari, and Silk Road would track them down long before help could arrive.

Elin lifted the Beretta she'd stolen from one of the guards. She lowered her window, leaned out, and took aim at their pursuers.

She shot at the other vehicle, and when more gunfire hit them, she ducked back inside.

"It's Claude's Land Rover. It's armored. I won't be able to take it out."

Hale knew their options were pretty limited. But there was no way he was letting Drift get his hands on Elin. "Take the wheel."

"What?" She looked at him incredulously. "Talk to me, Hale. What are you planning?"

"No time. We need to eliminate these guys. Give me the gun and you take the wheel." He held out a hand to her. "Keep it steady."

She stared at him for a beat, then more gunshots peppered their vehicle. Hale swerved and they were both tossed against their seats.

"Here." She slapped the Beretta into his hand. "Climb across."

She maneuvered over, practically sitting in his lap. Hale gripped her chin and turned her face to his. He pressed a hard kiss to her lips. "Whatever happens, you stay alive."

Her eyes flashed. "Hale—"

Reluctantly, he pulled away, sliding into the passenger seat. Their vehicle slowed, and more bullets shattered another window.

Elin settled behind the wheel, gunning the engine. Hale climbed out the side window, his upper body outside the vehicle, the wind tearing at him. He took aim and shot at the tires of the pursuing vehicle.

It wouldn't do much damage, since the vehicle had run-flat tires, but it might slow them down a bit.

The pursuing vehicle's engine roared as it charged closer.

Time for Plan B. "Get us alongside them," he yelled back at Elin.

She slowed their Land Rover and a second later, the Silk Road vehicle pulled up on their right. Hale climbed out onto the roof, staying crouched and holding onto the gear strapped to the vehicle to keep his balance. The wind made his eyes water.

"Hale!" Elin shouted from inside.

He looked over at the other vehicle. Then he stood and leaped onto the roof of the other Land Rover.

Chapter Nine

Oh, God. Hale had just *jumped* onto a moving vehicle.

Elin fell in behind the other four-wheel drive. She had a perfect view of Hale clinging to the Land Rover's roof.

The Silk Road driver started swerving from side to side, trying to shake Hale loose. With her heart in her throat, Elin watched, keeping pace. If Hale fell...

Come on, Hale. Let's see those superhuman SEAL skills.

She watched as he climbed across the roof. Then suddenly, he rolled to the side, almost sliding off the car completely. That's when she realized the Silk Road thugs were shooting upwards through the roof.

She had to do something. She revved, speeding right up to their bumper. She couldn't ram them and risk Hale falling. But maybe she could—

Bullets peppered her windshield and she ducked.

—distract them. She peered up, trying to keep right behind the other vehicle.

Hale was over the driver's side now, then he slipped over the edge, hanging upside down at the driver's side window. The SUV veered off the track and into the desert.

Elin slowed and watched Hale slide inside the vehicle, her heart trying to hammer its way out of her chest. She was known for her nerves of steel back in the office, but Hale Carter was testing her.

Suddenly, the vehicle stopped swerving, and did a wide turn. It headed back toward her.

Tense, she braked to a stop, and waited. The heavy tinting on the windows made it impossible to tell what was going on inside the vehicle.

The Land Rover pulled up beside her, and Hale opened the driver's side window and grinned at her.

Elin didn't stop to think. She threw the Land Rover into Park, slammed open her door, and stomped over to him.

"Do you have a death wish?" she yelled.

"Well, I—"

"Leaping from a moving vehicle? Onto *another* moving vehicle?" She watched as he opened the door and stepped out. Behind him, the bodies of two Silk Road guards were slumped motionless in their seats.

"Getting shot at," she continued. "Climbing into a car full of armed mercenaries out to kill you!"

"Well, there were only two—"

"Be quiet."

"Elin—"

She fisted a hand in his T-shirt and yanked him

forward. Then, she went up on her toes to press her mouth to his.

He was still for a second, then his mouth moved on hers, parting her lips. His tongue delved into her mouth. She reached up, gripping his shoulders. Desire shot through her like a bullet.

He took control of the kiss, and she liked it. The demanding sweep of his tongue, the way his big hands cupped her ass. She ground against him, needing more, needing to be closer.

Finally, they broke the kiss, both of them gasping for air.

"I'd do it again in a heartbeat, knowing that's what I'll get at the end."

She smacked his shoulder, still trying to get coherent thoughts to form.

"I'm fine," he murmured against her lips.

"Don't scare me like that again."

"Yes, ma'am." He ran a hand over her hair. "Now, let's put some distance between us and Silk Road."

Elin took some breaths and stepped back from him. "Sounds good. Let's see if there are any useful supplies or weapons in Claude's Land Rover, and then let's head west."

He shot her his trademark sexy smile, blinding her for a second. "And find a lost mine?"

"Sure, and let's find the mythical lost Seal of King Solomon while we're at it."

***

Hale stared into the side mirror. They'd been driving for hours across the flat desert, and hadn't seen any pursuers.

Looked like they'd gotten away.

Still, his muscles were tense, and he knew they were nowhere near to being safe. There was also the fact that there was no sign of a mountain or a mine.

Maybe there was no mine and no ring. Maybe this was all just a wild-goose chase that had cost people their lives.

"I can't believe Drift thinks the ring is some relic of a mythical advanced race," Elin muttered.

"Well, Zach...that's Dr. Zachariah James, he's Morgan's boyfriend."

"I've heard of him."

"He actually believes there were advanced civilizations that were flooded at the end of the last ice age."

Elin shot him a look.

"He's dived submerged structures that date to well before when man, as the current historical timeline allows, could have built them. He believes it's possible bits of their advanced technology may have survived."

Elin blew out a breath. "You believe that?"

"Hell, I've seen it. Our last mission in Madagascar...let's just say, I think it's very possible."

"I've seen things, too," she said quietly. "Including some classified files."

"So, there really could be a ring in King

Solomon's Mine that isn't magic, but is storing information about a whole lot of advanced technology?"

"I really hope not."

"I think it's time to contact Dec," Hale said, glancing over at Elin in the driver's seat.

Elin was silent for a second. "Do it."

He touched the small patch behind his ear. "Dec? You copy?"

Elin turned her head. "Anything?"

He shook his head.

"Dec, this is Hale. You receiving?"

"Hale?" Dec's voice, distorted by static. "We're receiving you. Where the hell are you? Are you and Elin okay?"

"We're okay, but the mission's gone to hell." Hale gave a succinct recap on everything that had happened.

"Wait," Dec said. "Did you say John Drift, the movie star? *He's* one of Silk Road's leaders?"

"Yep."

"Jesus. I always liked his movies. And now there's some other mystery player involved, who nearly killed you with an armed drone?"

"Yes."

"Great." There were a few unintelligible mutters. "Okay. How's Elin want to play this?"

Hale looked over at her. She looked calm, not like they'd just fought for their lives in the middle of the desert. He grinned. She was a hell of a woman. "Dec wants to know what your call is for the mission?"

Elin took her eyes off the road and glanced at him. "Have them on extraction standby. We'll give it another twenty-four hours, and if we haven't found the mine, we get out."

"And if we find the mine?"

"We'll call them and the government in to secure it."

Hale smiled. "And block Silk Road from having any access."

She smiled back. "That's the plan."

"I like the way you think." He relayed the plan to Dec.

"Acknowledged," Dec said. "But if Silk Road catches up with you again, or you hit any other problems, you contact us."

"You got it, Dec."

"Stay safe."

They kept driving toward the setting sun. Soon shadows were growing across the desert.

"How come you're out here in the hot desert, getting shot at?" he asked her.

"I always wanted to catch the bad guys. I grew up with a healthy respect for the rules, and for history. And you know about my father and my mother." She hunched her shoulders. "Besides, I'm good at it."

"I can see that."

Her shoulders relaxed. "Not everyone in my life has thought it was a good career for me."

"It's not for anyone else to decide, is it?"

"I like you, Hale."

"Feeling's mutual. So, why hasn't some

upwardly mobile guy snatched you up?"

"One did."

Hale blinked. She was *married?*

"It didn't stick." Her hands flexed on the wheel. "Apparently, I'm too involved with my work, and I didn't give him enough time and attention."

"Divorced?"

"Yes."

There were undercurrents in her tone. Hale guessed the breakdown of a marriage was never fun. Still, a part of him wanted to know if she still loved the idiot.

"And why hasn't some sweet, young thing snagged you?" Elin asked.

Hale looked out at the desert. "I'm...not a good bet."

"Oh? Gainfully employed, good guy, easy on the eyes."

"You know my last SEAL mission...went bad." He pressed cold hands against his thighs. "I came back messed up." He looked at her, saw her opening her mouth to speak. "I got therapy. I worked it out." At least the worst of it. "But I still have the nightmares, I still see the faces of the men I failed to save. Doesn't really make me a good prospect for sweet, young things. Besides, I prefer to keep things fun and casual."

"That makes two of us," Elin said. "It's getting dark. I think we'd better find somewhere to camp for the night."

Somewhere where Silk Road couldn't find them.

***

"Okay, I really can't see anything anymore," Elin said. She was tired and hungry, and the adrenaline from the day's chase was long gone.

The sun was almost gone, leaving a pitch-black desert, and only the slightest bit of light to the west. She couldn't risk using the headlights.

"Wait." Hale was leaning forward and staring out the windshield. "What the hell is that?"

Elin glanced off to the north. "Darkness, Carter. That's what happens when the sun sets."

"Look a little to the left, smart ass."

She did, and could just barely make out a massive shape in the darkness. She stiffened. *No way.*

A mountain rose up in the dark.

Hale tore open the glovebox, and pulled out a paper map. He folded it over, and spread it on his lap. He ran his finger over their location.

"If I'm calculating this right, we are about here."

She leaned over, looking at the map. "Looks right."

"There's no mountain on the map," Hale said. "It says it's flat here."

Elin frowned. "Mountains don't just appear from nowhere, Hale. Maybe we're off on our location."

"Based on where we camped last night, the direction we've traveled, and my calculation of our average speed, we're in the ballpark. Map says there are no mountains around here."

"Farini said they stumbled on a mountain, and

assumed it was the Ky Ky Mountains. But most people agree he was nowhere near the Ky Ky, and his guides didn't recognize it."

"Get us a bit closer."

Clenching the wheel and leaning forward, Elin did her best to drive them through the darkness. She pulled them to a stop at the rocky base of a large mountain.

They climbed out, staring up in the dark.

"Fancy a nighttime hike?" Hale reached in and pulled out their backpacks, ensuring they had some essentials.

She took her pack and slipped it on. "Sure, I love risking breaking my ankle while climbing in the dark." She pulled out her flashlight and clicked it on. "First, we need to hide the Land Rover. If Drift is looking for us from the air…"

Hale looked around. "Not many hiding places."

Elin pointed. "There's a rocky overhang there. It might squeeze under."

"It'll be a tight fit."

She jumped in and slowly eased the vehicle close to the overhang. As she drove underneath, rock screeched on metal, and she winced. When she climbed out, she studied it. "Not great, but it'll be less visible from the air." She turned to face the mountain.

They carefully hiked up the rocky hill. There were no structures, or rock walls. Nothing to indicate this was the Lost City of the Kalahari, Ophir, or the entrance to King Solomon's Mines.

She followed Hale, wondering if this mission was

going to end with her emptyhanded.

"Look," Hale breathed.

Elin lifted her light and saw a giant archway of stone appear out of the darkness. Her mouth dropped open. *Incredible.*

The two of them stopped beneath it. It was in good condition. She shone her light across the stone.

She instantly saw the engravings.

"Damn, I wish I had my tablet." But as she stared at these symbols, she realized it was a language she didn't recognize at all.

"Pretty sure we're in the right place." Hale pointed directly above them.

In the center of the arch was the Star of David symbol.

"Jesus," Elin said. "This is Ophir."

They walked under the arch, and she felt a wild fizz of excitement in her blood. Ahead, more ruins appeared. Rows of large columns. They'd tumbled down long ago, but the bases still stood, sturdy and proud. A reminder of the long-ago grandeur of this place.

They walked through the center row of columns. "This looks like it was some sort of temple."

"Must have been incredible in its day," Hale murmured.

They reached the end, and found themselves staring at a high rock wall that had been carved from the mountainside. Along it was a row of large doorways. Each doorway was covered in a slab of rock.

"There are some engravings here." Hale shone his light on the wall.

Elin stared at them. "There's the Star of David again. Hey, this symbol looks Phoenician."

"What's it mean?"

She looked at him. "Death."

"Great."

"I think this is a test. Only one door is the correct entrance to the mines. If you get the wrong one, it means death."

"Really great," Hale muttered.

Elin stared hopelessly at the text on the wall. "Hale, I can't translate this."

"Maybe you don't have to."

"How are we going to pick the right door?"

Hale stalked along the wall, with his flashlight aimed at the ground, not the doors. She followed with a frown. When he reached the end, he turned and moved back to one doorway.

"This is it."

"How do you know?" she asked.

"Look." He aimed his flashlight down.

That's when Elin saw it. The ground was worn, impressions carved into the stone from what could only be long use. The ancient tracks of heavy carts, people, and animals moving through here. A quick glance showed the other thresholds didn't have the same wear.

"You're brilliant!" she said.

"I know."

"And humble." She grabbed his hand and squeezed.

Together, they moved closer to the door. Hale paused to study what looked like the locking mechanism. He touched a hand to it.

There was a rumble, and, a moment later, the slab of rock covering the doorway slid open. Elin stared at the yawning hole of darkness leading into the mountain.

"I need to call Dec," he said, awe in his voice.

"Tell him to arrive in the morning to secure the mines. In the meantime, we'll look for the Seal of Solomon."

Hale quickly touched his ear, and Elin listened as he spoke with his boss. She peered into the dark mine and wondered just what they were going to find inside.

"Okay, Dec said to stay safe, and he'll see us tomorrow. He's also updating Burke."

"Great." She waved a hand at Hale. "After you."

"How about we go together?"

She nodded, and when he took her hand, she linked her fingers with his. Together, they entered the mines of Ophir.

Chapter Ten

Hale and Elin's footsteps echoed through the dark tunnel. He aimed the flashlight upward, studying the rough rock. "This looks natural."

"I wouldn't be surprised if the people who created the mines made use of any natural systems of tunnels through here." She was looking at the floor. "There are grooves worn in the floor here, too. It has to be from mining carts."

"Look." Hale paused, his light aimed at the wall.

Elin hurried over, her fingers touching the Star of David symbol carved into the rock. "I can hardly believe we've found the legendary Ophir. King Solomon's Mines."

"You think an all-powerful ring is waiting for us in here somewhere?" Hale asked.

"I hope not."

They kept moving, heading deeper into the mine. The tunnels changed, the walls and ceiling becoming more regular. Side tunnels snaked off the main tunnel, at regular intervals.

They reached a junction.

"Which way?" he asked.

"That way." Elin pointed to where the Star of David symbol was carved on the wall. As the tunnel system got more complex, they continued to follow the symbols.

Soon, the tunnels morphed into very straight walls and flat, paved floors, that were definitely man-made. It was amazing to think that thousands of years ago, man had carved these, all in the hunt for gold and diamonds.

"Oh, my God." Elin hurried forward. "Look at this."

Her light illuminated a section of tunnel that looked different from what they'd seen so far. These incredible carvings were images, not text. They were all carved deep into the stone, and some had once been painted, though over time the colors had deteriorated from age and the underground conditions.

The two of them slowed their pace, staring at the amazing pictures. Detailed scenes depicted the mining work, carts being pulled, workers using pickaxes. Others showed the smelting of the gold, the molten metal being scooped up from large, stone tubs carved into the rock. Many of the workers resembled the local San people, with small, wiry statures and short hair. But a few of the people also looked a little different—taller with longer hair.

Hale frowned. Were these people the enigmatic survivors of a pre-flood race?

Some images showed the lives of the miners. San families crowded around a beautiful lake and waterfall—people eating, children playing.

It made Hale think of the Okavango Delta in

Botswana. It wasn't too far from here. "This area must have been wetter back then."

Elin nodded. "Come on. Let's keep moving."

They continued through the twists and turns of the tunnels. Hale kept an eye out for any booby traps. He wasn't expecting rolling boulders, but he'd heard tales of poisoned arrows, and knew the San people were excellent hunters.

He'd expected the place to be better protected...even after being abandoned for centuries.

They rounded a corner and Hale sucked in a breath.

Ahead, part of the tunnel had collapsed. They got closer to the pile of rocks, and Hale studied the roof. "Be careful. It doesn't look very stable in places."

Elin cautiously moved forward, lifting her flashlight to shine on the unstable roof.

Then she pitched forward.

In a flash, Hale realized the blackness ahead of her wasn't a rock wall...it was a huge, gaping hole in the floor.

He lunged forward and grabbed her. As he yanked her back, she dropped her flashlight, and both of them fell to the ground. They watched the glow of her spinning flashlight, as it fell down a huge, cylindrical shaft.

"Thanks," she said, her voice raspy, her fingers gripping him.

They waited and, moments later, heard a clatter as her light finally hit the bottom. Carefully, Hale moved closer to the edge, and shone his beam of light down.

The giant cylindrical hole speared down into the heart of the mine. He couldn't see the bottom; the light had been swallowed by the dense darkness. He looked up, and near where part of the roof had collapsed, the rotting wooden remains of what looked like a pulley mechanism was attached to the wall.

"This is a man-made shaft. There's some sort of lift mechanism there, although it's mostly ruined."

She nodded. "Just like a modern-day mine. This would have been the main access, up and down."

He cautiously tested the edge. "This side of the shaft looks more stable."

Elin looked over. "Can we climb down there?"

Hale pulled his backpack off. "I have some basic climbing gear." He always carried his lightweight ropes and harnesses on a mission.

"In your bag of tricks?"

"Yep."

"Well, we might not need them." She pointed down one side of the shaft. "There's a narrow path cut into the side here. It spirals downward."

"We caught a break."

"First time for everything." She started down the rocky path, keeping her hands pressed to the rock wall. "It's narrow. And crumbling in places, so be careful."

"Here." He tossed her his flashlight, and then followed her, carefully placing his boot with each step and testing the rock beneath. He peered down into the darkness. He did *not* want to fall.

All of a sudden, the sound of rock scraping on rock broke the silence. He looked over his shoulder...

A huge block of rock thrust out of the wall, like a piston, then retracted.

What the hell? He barely had time to comprehend what was happening, before another block rushed out in front of him. It caught his side, knocking him off balance. "Fuck! Elin, watch out!"

He heard Elin curse, but he was too busy teetering on the edge of the path. He felt his weight tip toward the gaping hole of the shaft.

A hand grabbed his arm, yanking him back toward the wall. Hale pressed his body against the rock, sucking in air.

"Okay?" Elin was right beside him.

"Yeah. Thanks." He blew out a breath. "Don't move. There's some kind of booby trap built into the wall."

She raised the flashlight, and he could just make out the joints showing where the moving blocks were hidden, all along the wall ahead. They ran on into the darkness.

"Dammit," she muttered. "We can't play Russian roulette with these traps. We have to find another way." She aimed the light downward.

"Hey, what's that?" He crouched, touching just over the edge of the path.

She angled the light better. "It looks like handholds cut into the rock. It's a ladder down."

"Right, or another trap," he said darkly.

"We have to try." She wedged the flashlight up her sleeve. "I'll go first."

Elin went backward over the edge, slotting her boots into the handholds. She moved downward cautiously. Hale unzipped his bag, ready to go for his grappling gun if anything happened to her.

She paused and looked up. "It seems fine. Sturdy, and no signs of any joints that indicate a booby trap."

Hale grunted. He still didn't like it. He climbed over the edge and followed her down.

"Now we've caught a break," she called up.

"I don't recommend saying that."

"Don't tell me you're superstitious, I didn't—" Her voice broke off.

"Elin?"

"Ah, we might have a problem."

"What?" He moved down until he was just above her.

"Shit, it's starting to feel warm." She lifted one hand. "These handholds are covered in something wet. I thought it was water." She gasped. "God, Hale, it's starting to burn."

He caught a glimpse of dark-green sludge on her hand. "It's some sort of poison. We need to wash it off."

The flashlight bobbed. "There's a ledge just down a bit farther." Her voice was tight with pain.

Hale watched her climb down and then he moved as far as he could without touching the poisoned handholds, then dropped the last few feet to the ledge, landing beside her.

She was already grabbing her water bottle. She doused one hand. "It's sticky. It won't come off!"

Hale heard the strain in her voice. He shoved a hand over his shoulder, and grabbed a cloth from his bag. She held her hand up and he swiped the gunk off and then poured some of his own water over her hand.

"Better?"

"Yes. I think it's blistering, but it's not burning anymore."

Hale fished out his small first aid kit. "Let me see it." Gently, he studied the blisters and rubbed some antiseptic cream on her skin. He covered them with a bandage.

She looked up at him. "Now what?"

"Now we rappel down."

She nodded. "Let's do it."

Hale pulled out the harnesses and handed one to her.

She studied the gear. "This is the smallest, lightest climbing harness I've ever seen."

"My own design." He maneuvered into his. "I wanted basic, lightweight gear I could take on missions. Just in case of an emergency."

He grabbed his tools and banged hooks into the rock. They double checked each other's ropes and tied on.

He looked down into the cavernous darkness. "Nice day for a climb."

She gave a strangled laugh and then started downward, her boots pressed to the rock.

***

Elin had always loved rappelling. Early in her marriage, she and Matthew had taken their gear and headed out to climb in the Shenandoah National Park. She hadn't been in a long time.

But she couldn't say rappelling in complete darkness was much fun.

She paused for a second, swiping her arm across her face. The deeper they went, the hotter it got. Her shirt was damp with sweat. And her left hand was still stinging from whatever the hell that poison had been.

Beside her, Hale moved with easy, athletic grace. She hadn't expected anything less. It was clear he'd done plenty of climbing. In fact, he looked like he was enjoying himself.

"We've gone a long way down," she said.

He nodded. "I still can't see the bottom, but we must be getting close."

Good. She didn't want to run into any more booby traps. They kept moving downward, and Elin hoped their ropes were long enough.

"Let's take a break." She hung from her rope and pulled her water bottle off her backpack. She tipped it back and drank. Beside her, Hale did the same.

The flashlight was still tucked in her sleeve and was aiming at the rock wall. She spotted something. Clipping her water bottle back on, she pressed her hand to the rock and pulled herself closer. "There's something here."

Hale tensed. "Another trap?"

Frowning, she pressed her fingers into the grooves. "At first glance, I thought they were engravings, but they're not. I don't see any poison." She fingered one. They were a bunch of long lines cut into the rock.

Suddenly, a silver blade flashed out of one of the long grooves. Elin yanked her hand back and darted to the side. She caught a glimpse of a silver circle shoot out into the darkness.

"What the hell!" Hale yelled.

"It was some sort of blade." God, another booby trap.

Another blade flashed out, catching Elin's rope. It nicked the line, and she dropped downward a few inches.

"Hold on, Elin." Hale's voice was hard and tense.

"Stay away from the grooves." She swung her flashlight up and her gut cramped. Her rope was fraying.

The rope let go some more and she dropped another few inches. Her rope was almost completely frayed through. She pressed her hands to the rock face, avoiding the blade grooves and looking for a handhold. Anything.

There was nothing but smooth rock. "There's nothing to hold on to!"

"Hold on, dammit." Hale was rummaging in his backpack.

Her rope broke. Elin dropped, a scream caught in her throat.

Suddenly, she jerked to a halt, her right arm

wrenching. Hale had grabbed her wrist. His face was set in harsh lines above her.

"Hold...on," he ground out.

Elin tried not to move, but she felt her hand slipping through his. "Hale." She didn't want to die.

"Trust me, Elin."

Her hand slipped some more. Trust was something Elin wasn't good at. But the time she'd spent with Hale had shown her that he was a loyal man who fought for what was right. "I do."

Her fingers slipped from his. All the air rushed out of her as she fell, and time seemed to move in slow motion.

She saw Hale lift something. There was a *thwap* sound, and she saw something streak out over her head.

Then she watched as Hale unclipped his harness and leaped out into the shaft after her.

Horror filled her. "Hale, no!"

His big body slammed into her. She found her face smashed against his chest, one of his arms wrapped around her.

"Hold on!" he yelled.

She did, and the next second, they were swinging across the shaft. Hale lifted his legs and a second later, his boots hit the other wall, absorbing the force of their swing.

They hung there for a moment, both of them breathing hard.

Elin swallowed and looked up. He was holding the smallest grappling gun she'd ever seen. The line disappeared into the darkness above them.

"Well, it worked," he said. "Shit. Let's not do that again."

She gripped onto him, wrapping her legs around his hips. He reached between them, clipping a spare carabiner onto her harness, tying them together.

"Shit. Shit." He tangled a hand in her hair and pulled her close, his face pressed to the side of her neck.

Elin held on, liking the soothing beat of his heart beneath her ear, even if his heartbeat was racing a little. Her own was jumping all over the place.

"Okay?" His breath was warm against her cheek.

She nodded. "Just need a second."

His arms tightened on her. "Hell, I need a month or two."

She managed a choked laugh. "Thanks for catching me."

"Always." His hand cupped her cheek, tilting her face up to his. "I'll reach for you, come for you, rescue you anytime you need it. You need someone to fight by your side, I'll be there."

Elin felt something inside her shudder and bloom. When things were good with her ex, it had been fun and companionable, but it was only now she realized Matthew wouldn't have put himself out for her or risked his life. He wouldn't have fought beside her, or come for her when she needed him.

She stared into Hale's handsome, shadowed face

and saw a strong warrior who would never let her down. Now she felt something else in her chest...something bigger, bolder, and far scarier than she'd ever felt before.

Hale pressed a quick kiss to her lips. "Ready to keep going?"

She nodded. He pressed something on the grappling gun and they started to lower downward again. It was awkward with them clipped together, but they managed. When Elin's boots touched a gravelly bottom, she let out a long breath.

They unclipped and Hale retracted the grappling gun rope. She shone her flashlight around. There was an arched doorway set in the rock wall, and below their feet, the ground was damp.

They moved toward the arch. It was cut perfectly into the rock and covered with amazing carvings. More images of the mine workers going about their work.

Together, Elin and Hale stepped into the tunnel, gravel crunching underfoot.

"Wait." Hale grabbed her arm.

Wary of more booby traps, she stopped.

"There are alcoves set into the wall. Shine the light over there."

Gold glinted in the darkness. Elin gasped and hurried forward. The alcove was stacked with rough bars of gold. "Oh, my God."

"These must have been storage areas...for before the gold was shipped out." He moved to the next alcove. There were more stacked gold bars.

Elin picked a bar up. They were larger than a

modern bar and rougher in form. They were stamped with the Star of David. "Just amazing. Some worker dug the gold-laden rock from the ground, smelted it, and made this."

"You really do care about the history," Hale said.

She looked up at him. "Of course. My earliest memories are of listening to my mom talk about the history and provenance of the artwork she was restoring. She told me that history shows us where we've been, and the heart of who we are. It also gives us hope about where we're going and who we can become."

"Sounds like a wise woman."

Elin smiled. "She'd like you. My mother has a thing for young, hot men." When Hale's eyebrows rose, Elin laughed. "Mom would tell you she has excellent taste in all things." Elin shone the light closer to his face. "Are you blushing?"

"Ex-Navy SEALs don't blush."

With another laugh, Elin headed farther down the tunnel, Hale a step behind her. A moment later, it opened up. She lifted the flashlight. It was a huge, dome-like cavern.

Elin gasped. There was a large lake of water, with a small waterfall running down one rock wall. A carpet of moss-like plants grew along the side of the water. Several cylindrical rock pillars extended up to the roof, many of which were covered in trailing plants.

"How are there plants down here?" she said.

He reached out and touched a vine draped over some rocks. "They look like moss, so they've adapted to the low light." He shook his head. "They must get some light down here. I've never seen anything like them before."

But something else caught Elin's attention. She strode toward the pool and stopped at the edge, crouching down to snatch up a rock.

It was a white opaque color. And it wasn't a rock.

She spun. "Hale, look."

He gripped her wrist, turning it to study the rock in the light.

"It's an uncut diamond," he breathed.

They looked around. Similar, opaque rocks of all sizes dotted the gravel floor. All uncut diamonds.

"This is amazing," she breathed.

Hale gave a shake of his head. "I don't just think we found Ophir. I think we just found the Bushman's Paradise, as well."

Chapter Eleven

Hale crouched and scooped fresh water onto his face and down his arms. Behind him, Elin was pacing.

"The Bushman's Paradise. Ophir. King Solomon's Mines. The Lost City of the Kalahari." She spun to face him. "They're all the same thing."

"It's not surprising," he said. "All the myths and stories in this one desolate place had to center on something."

Elin paced again, running her hand through her hair. "And somewhere in here is Solomon's ring."

They'd searched the cavern the best they could, and hadn't found any other ways in or out. They had found rock-cut houses gouged into the back wall, more moss-like plants, and even several small artifacts that proved people had once lived here.

"Elin, shut it down for a bit. Come and wash that hand."

She stopped beside him and he carefully dunked her hand in the water. The tinkle of the waterfall was a soothing backdrop noise. Hale studied her palm. It was pink in places, and she had a couple of blisters, but otherwise, it looked okay.

She looked tired, with dark circles under her

eyes. He knew it was late and they needed some rest.

"Let's camp in one of the houses," she said.

He watched her glance at the far wall of the cavern. It was draped in more moss-like plants, with arched doorways. The cave houses were all rectangular, and evenly spaced out.

Elin stood with the flashlight and strode around the pool. She stopped by the wall, and before he caught up to her, she stepped inside one of the caves.

"Elin!" He followed her in.

"Amazing to think the workers lived here," she murmured.

Furniture had been carved out of the rock, and here and there, he saw broken ceramics and remnants of rotted fabrics. He picked up a small figure carved from bone. A toy, maybe? "Layne, Dec's fiancée, would love to check this place out. And Cal's girlfriend Dani would spend hours photographing the place."

Elin glanced over her shoulder. "And Dec and Cal's parents would like it, too."

"Oh, yeah. Professor Ward would want to record every inch of it and Mrs. Ward..."

Elin's lips twitched. "I know what infamous treasure hunters like to do."

"She isn't like Silk Road. She trades antiquities legitimately." Mostly.

The house was made of several rooms for living, sleeping, and storage. They stepped into the back room, and found a stone platform topped with a pile of what had to have been rotted furs. A bed, probably.

"It's like they just left," she said. "Just got up and walked out." She dropped onto the platform.

"Elin, we need to rest." He looked at his watch. "It's late, and we've had a hell of a day. Why don't you wash up, and I'll organize some dinner? For tonight, this can be our place." He pulled the small battery-powered lantern out of his bag.

With a nod, she wandered out and down to the water. Layne would probably kill him for sleeping on historical artifacts, but he shoved the dust of the rotted furs aside and laid out their sleeping bags. He started pulling things out of their backpacks. They had a few ready-to-eat meals, and some packs of biltong. Not gourmet, but it would do.

Outside, he heard a splash of water, and he froze. His overheated imagination had no problem imagining Elin naked. That pale skin with a hint of gold, those tantalizing curves, and all that blonde hair. Yeah, he could easily imagine his darker hands smoothing up toned thighs, over a taut belly, tangling in golden strands of hair as he pulled that pretty mouth closer to—

He muttered a curse, shifting to accommodate his hardening cock. Jeez, they'd survived a wild, dangerous day, were now in the bowels of a legendary mine, and something told him Silk Road wouldn't have given up searching for them. This was no time for dirty thoughts. Clearing his throat, he set the food out.

He heard water splashing again, and this time,

the urge to look was too great. He moved out of the rock-cut house and looked down at the pool, only a few feet away. Instantly, his cock was hard as a rock. She was waist-deep in the water, illuminated by the flashlight, and he had the perfect view of a slim, bare back, and the top curves of her ass.

With a groan, he turned away. *Focus on something else, Carter.* He moved back to their backpacks. How the hell was he going to sleep with her so close to him?

When Elin returned, she was wearing her cargo pants and a clean tank top. Her hair was damp and hung past her shoulders. He'd never seen it loose before.

"Your turn." She dumped her things. "The water isn't warm, but it's not too cold, either."

He grunted and headed to the pool. Cold would be welcome right now.

Hale kept it quick. He stripped off and strode into the water. The water did feel good. He stared down at his hard cock and grimaced. The water didn't do much to help that problem. Finally, he strode out and pulled on his last set of clean clothes.

Back in the house, he saw Elin munching on their meager dinner. Dropping down next to her, he snatched up some food. "We'll sleep for a few hours, then search for the ring. Our ride out of here will be here in the morning."

"I'm going to search for Drift, Hale. I can't let him get away."

"I figured you'd say something like that." Hale

smiled, chewing some biltong. "It's been a hell of a vacation. Next time, I suggest the mountains." When he looked up, he saw that she was watching him with a steady gaze.

Hell, she was beautiful. At first glance, she looked so cool, but there was heart and heat under the glossy exterior. Elin Alexander was a smart woman with a sense of passion and dedication to her job that he loved.

They stared at each other, gazes locking.

Hale wasn't sure who moved first. He was reaching for her and suddenly she was diving into his lap. She straddled him, her hands bunching in his T-shirt. Together, they tore it over his head.

"God. I've wanted to touch this chest for so long. It's been driving me crazy." She stroked her hands up his pecs. "All these muscles."

Hale was just as desperate. He pulled her tank top up, peeling it over her skin. Beneath, she was wearing a sports bra that only took him seconds to yank off. He cupped her full breasts, loving the way the plump curves fit into his palms.

"I'm going to touch you, kiss you, taste you," Hale ground out. "I want you to come on my fingers, on my tongue, and on my cock."

"Really?" A smile hovered on her lips. "Well, I have plans to make you come, too. I wonder who can make the other come first?"

Excitement shot through him. A challenge. "Game on, Agent Alexander. Just so you know, my last test was clean and I always use protection." A look crossed his face. "Which I don't have with me."

"It's okay. I'm healthy, too, and I get a regular contraceptive shot."

Hale shaped her rib cage and pulled her closer, until her breasts were level with his face. He pulled one pink nipple into his mouth. She moaned, her hands tangling in his hair. He sucked hard, then blew over the sensitive peak, loving the way it pebbled for him, and loving the way she writhed against him. He moved over to the other breast, giving the other pretty nipple some attention.

Soon, she was undulating against him, and he kept lavishing attention on her breasts. Damn, if he'd known just how gorgeous they were, he'd never have made it this far into the desert without already sampling them. God, she was so responsive to his touch.

A moment later, he felt her hands lower on his body, brushing against his stomach. He sucked in a breath.

She flicked open his trousers and a hand slid inside. When she brushed against his cock, he jerked.

"You like me touching you," she murmured.

"Hell, yes."

She moved back enough to pull his cock out. It was hard and engorged. "I've thought about seeing this, touching this." Her gaze flicked up to his. "Very impressive, Mr. Carter."

She stroked him, and Hale jerked and groaned.

"I want to make you feel good, Hale." She scooted back, pushed him back onto the sleeping bags, and lowered her head.

Her blonde hair fell around her face like a curtain. Desperate to see, he pushed it back and watched as she wrapped her lips around the fat head of his cock.

"Fuck...Elin." He couldn't think. Only feel.

Every one of his muscles bunched, and he felt the swirl of her tongue before she sucked him deep.

"You taste amazing, Hale." She licked around the mushroom head of his cock, her gaze locking with his. "You like watching me while I suck you?"

His hand clenched in her hair. "Yes."

She sucked him into her mouth again, her cheeks hollowing. Sensation shot through him and he rolled his hips up, watching her take more of him.

Hell. If she kept this up, he'd spill in her mouth in seconds. He wanted more, needed more.

Moving fast, he reared up.

"Hey!" she complained.

"You put your clever mouth on my cock again, I'll be coming down your throat."

She made a frustrated noise, but using his superior strength, he stripped her trousers off.

"That was the point," she said huskily. "I like to win."

He spun her around so she was on her knees. He moved up behind her, wrapping his arms around her until he cupped her breasts again. "My turn to tease you." He stroked his hand down her belly and felt her muscles quiver. "Yeah, that's right, Elin. My turn to have you whimpering."

He brushed his fingers through the trimmed

blonde curls between her legs.

"Hale." She was moving urgently now, her bare ass rubbing against his throbbing cock. He wouldn't be able to prove his stamina now, not if he splashed his come all over the small of her back.

He focused on pleasuring her, sliding his fingers through her folds. His hand was drenched in her slick juices, and he slid one finger inside her warmth. Damn, she was tight.

Her head fell back against his shoulder, her hips riding his hand. He slid another finger inside her, stretching her. He moved his thumb into her folds and found her clit.

She cried out, her back arching against him.

"I like to win too, baby," he murmured against her ear. "I'm going to make you come on my fingers, Elin."

"No." Determination filled her tone. She rubbed her ass against him and his cock slid between her rounded cheeks. He groaned, his head falling forward so he pressed his face against her hair.

She worked herself up and down, his cock sliding against smooth skin. He thumbed her clit and she tried hard to stifle her cry.

"Come inside me, Hale. I want your big cock inside me."

Damn. He'd never guessed there was a temptress under Elin's sleek exterior. "You come first." He pressed a third finger into her and knew she'd feel the stretch.

She was panting now, her ass still moving against him. "But I need your cock inside me, stretching me, filling me." She turned her head, her lips meeting his in a frantic kiss. "Don't you want to watch as you thrust inside me?"

Her words were like a red cape to a bull. Desperate now, he spun her, pressing her back against their makeshift bed. "I want that. More than anything. I've never been with a woman without a condom." He leaned over her, letting his gaze skate down her body, taking in every curve. "So fucking beautiful."

She let her pale legs fall open. "Hale, hurry up."

He shoved his trousers down to his knees. He took his cock, pumping it a few times. Her gaze was glued to it and she licked her lips.

"I'm going to stretch you out and make you come," he said on a growl.

"Yes."

He shoved her legs wider apart, and pressed the head of his cock against her warm dampness. He held himself there, every muscle in his body quivering. "Watch."

She pushed up on her elbows, her gaze where his thick cock looked big against her smooth skin.

Hale kept his gaze on her face and, with one firm thrust, lodged himself inside her.

***

God, Elin pressed her head back against the sleeping bag, she was so full.

Hale pulled back, sliding out of her and making her moan. Her gaze flew to him, and she watched as he thrust back inside her again. The look on his face made her breath catch. Like he'd found a heaven he'd never experienced before.

He soon found his rhythm, hammering inside her. She reached up, gripping his hard biceps, breathy cries exploding from her throat. He surrounded her, and dominated her, and it felt so good.

God, his body was a work of art, and she loved seeing the flex of muscles in his stomach, the air pumping in and out of his chest as he fucked her. By now, they were both slick with sweat, grinding against each other.

Sensations were rolling inside her and she knew it wouldn't take much for her to come. She squeezed her inner muscles and heard Hale groan.

"I'm going to make you come first," she said.

His heavy thrusts never faltered. "So competitive."

"Don't you forget it." She smiled. "God, you're so big, Hale. I love you inside me."

"Baby, you keep talking like that and it's going to get rougher and harder."

She felt her belly contract. "Promise?"

She was rewarded with another groan. Soon, neither of them could talk anymore, both lost in the torrent of heat rushing through them. He was thrusting hard into her, and she was straining up against him, desperate for more.

Elin was fighting to keep her orgasm from crashing over her. She could feel he was getting close as well.

Then he moved, sliding a hand down her body, and she felt his rough thumb slide over her slippery clit.

Elin was thrown over the edge. She bit her lip to stifle her scream as she came, and at the same time, her release triggered his. His hands clenched on her hips, dragging her up to meet his hard and now-erratic thrusts. He slammed into her one last time, lodging deep. His body shook as he poured himself inside her with a ragged groan.

Elin collapsed back, sure she'd never be able to move again. Hale dropped heavily beside her, one leg tossed over hers. She looked at his face, now relaxed, and still far too handsome. But she knew that under the tough good looks was a good man.

"Jesus," he said, breathless.

She smiled, her hot skin cooling a little.

"Elin, that was..."

"Yeah." She pressed her face to his shoulder. "It was."

She couldn't find the right words, either. After thirty-three years, she'd finally had the kind of sex she'd only ever read about. She'd always thought her love life had been decent enough, but after what she and Hale had just done...

Hale shifted, and she found herself being picked up. She slid an arm over his shoulders. "How can you even move?"

"Navy SEAL strength and stamina, darlin'." He stopped to dip and grab the flashlight.

He carried her out to the water, set the flashlight down to point toward the pool, then strode straight in. The water hit her and she let out a squeak. It felt even cooler now, on her overheated skin. He set her down, and she ducked down into the water. After days in the desert, she enjoyed feeling clean again.

When she surfaced, she looked at Hale and just stared.

She'd never, ever get tired of looking at that amazing body of his. Rivulets of water were running down his dark skin, arrowing down to a cock that looked big even when it wasn't hard.

"See anything you like?"

His amused drawl made her look up. "Have I told you that you have an unreal body? I mean, most FBI agents keep fit, but you..."

He made a scoffing sound. "So, I work out. Lots of guys do."

"Yeah, but you look like you're ready for war."

"Habit, I guess." He splashed more water onto his chest. "Plus, my THS missions aren't always easy. I need to be fit."

She kept staring at him, and heat washed through her, settling in her belly. "I want you again."

His head snapped up, his eyes narrowing and nostrils flaring. Like a male who'd scented a female in heat.

She knew they'd need to start searching for the ring soon...but right now, they needed to rest and recharge. And nothing had ever made her feel more energized than Hale Carter touching her.

He took two strides to reach her, churning

through the water. He yanked her up into his arms. As his hands cupped her ass and lifted her up, she wound her legs around his hips, gripping his hard shoulders.

She loved that he held her so easily with that strength of his. She reached between them and found his cock. It was hard and pulsed in her hand. It took a second to line him up, and then she was sinking down on him, feeling the fat head slide into her. *God.* She bit down on her lip, air rushing past her lips. She took him, inch by inch, inside her.

He muttered a curse. Elin started working herself up and down on his cock, and he helped, his fingers digging into the flesh of her ass.

Her husky cries echoed around them, mixing with Hale's deeper groans. He was so big and she felt stretched to her limits. It hurt, but it felt good, too.

Suddenly, Hale strode out of the pool and toward their borrowed house, still holding her impaled on his cock.

He made it to the bedroom and dropped to his knees on the sleeping bags. He grinned at her. "Let's see who comes first this time."

Chapter Twelve

Hale woke, holding a naked Elin in his arms. His internal alarm clock had woken him. As a SEAL, he'd learned to fall asleep fast and anywhere, and to 'set' himself to wake in a few hours. It was a skill that still proved useful.

The sun would just be rising, so Dec and the others would be getting ready to head their way. Just a couple more hours and their rescue would arrive.

He breathed deep, holding her tight. Once again, he'd slept soundly with Elin wrapped around him. She was his shield against the nightmares.

She could be hard and tough, and so damn smart, but under his hands, she could be soft, as well. He couldn't believe that her idiot ex had let her go. His hold tightened. The guy's loss was Hale's gain.

Mine now. He stroked his hand down her smooth skin. *Mine.*

Damn. For the first time ever, Hale wanted to keep a woman. He waited to see if he'd break out in his usual sweat, or for his pulse to start racing. Nope, nothing. Just a warm glow inside him, and a knowledge that he wanted Elin in his life. He realized he'd been letting the horrors of his past keep him from letting people too close. He'd been using his pain as a barrier between him and the world.

He knew it hurt to lose the people you loved, so he'd not let anyone close. Now, his next challenge was convincing the woman herself to give them a chance.

He was a smart guy. He was up for the challenge. But first, they had a treasure to find and a mission to finish.

Noises. Hale tensed and turned his head. Faint echoes.

Fuck. It was voices.

"Elin," he murmured, shaking her.

"Hmm." She stretched against him, turning her head to press a kiss to his chest.

"Someone's coming," he said.

She snapped awake, her eyes clearing of sleep. She cocked her head, and he watched her stiffen as she heard the sounds.

She leaped to her feet and searched for her clothes. "Do you think it's our team?"

Hale had learned to listen to his instincts. "It's too early. They'll be here in another hour or two. Besides, we wouldn't hear Dec coming. My guess is its Drift and his buddies."

"Silk Road never gives up." She buttoned her trousers. "Damn, I can't find my T-shirt."

Hale quickly pulled on his trousers. "Grab one of mine. Quick."

She pulled one of his T-shirts out of his bag, and yanked it on. It was too big, but she knotted the bottom and then pulled her loose khaki top over the top and buttoned it. As he shoved the rest of their things back into their packs and rolled up their sleeping bags, he watched her tuck her shirt into her trousers.

He was sorry to see all Elin's sexy curves covered, and her FBI agent demeanor back in place. Once this was over, he promised he'd take his time with her. Explore every inch of her—touch her with his hands, his tongue, everything.

He handed her a backpack. "Come on, we need to get into the tunnel before they block our only exit out of here."

As they moved out of the cave house, he realized he could see a golden light ahead.

"What the hell?" Elin breathed.

They reached the doorway. The entire cavern was lit with golden light.

"How is there light?" She arched her head, looking toward the soaring ceiling above.

Hale looked up at the arched roof. "I'm not sure. I can see some gold panels up there. My guess is they have some sort of lighting system." Excitement rushed through him. He'd kill to know what ingenious methods the ancient miners had developed. "Maybe using reflected light from the surface? I'd need to see it up close to know for sure."

She flashed him a quick smile. "I like when your geek side shows."

Another echo of voices and they both stiffened. "Come on. Let's get back to the tunnel."

They crept through the cavern. As they neared the tunnel, the voices got louder. *Shit.* They were close.

Hale heard a distinctive, deep voice. Drift.

"Find them." The man's voice echoed off the walls. "I want the Seal of Solomon, and I want the spies dead. Kill them."

Hale grabbed Elin's arm and pulled her back into the cavern. He skirted the water. "We need to find another way out of here."

"There's no other way out. We looked."

"There must be something." He looked around the underground paradise. "We need to find the Seal of Solomon before Drift. And no way am I planning to die today."

They moved along the walls, searching. Suddenly, Elin paused. "I feel airflow."

He moved up beside her, and felt the faint brush of air on his skin. "I feel it, too." He pushed aside some of the mossy vines. Solid rock lay behind them.

On the other side of the cavern, he heard the Silk Road team enter from the tunnel.

Adrenaline charged through him. Any second now, they'd spot Hale and Elin.

"No joints or openings," she murmured, running her hands over the rock.

Dammit. He pressed his hands against the rock. That air had to be coming from somewhere.

Suddenly, rock moved beneath his hands. A

small square of rock depressed inward, and Hale stepped back.

"Elin?"

"I see it. Maybe it's a—"

A second later, the floor beneath them fell away. Hale fell down a small set of steps, Elin tumbling right behind him and ramming into his back.

He looked up...just in time to see the rock trap door above sliding closed, locking them in impenetrable darkness.

***

Elin fumbled around in her backpack and found the flashlight Hale had given her. She flicked it on.

They were in a narrow tunnel. The walls had more carvings on them, and in this tunnel, the beautiful, multicolored paint had been preserved. The vibrant colors were stunning.

They both stood, and Elin dusted off her trousers. She walked over to the closest wall, her gaze on the images.

"Okay, Layne would give her firstborn child to see this," Hale said.

Elin shone the light around. "Hopefully, she'll get the chance, without giving away any of her children."

"We have to get out of here, first."

She heard the word he didn't say. *Alive*. They had to get out of there alive.

Well, she sure wasn't letting Silk Road kill them. Her gaze skated across the images, then moved back and zeroed in on one. "Hale, what does that look like to you?"

He moved up beside her. "Hell. A ring."

The image showed a man in golden robes with a long beard holding a small object above his head. It was a bulky ring with a large stone in the center. The stone was set in the middle of a star.

They walked down the tunnel, Elin staring at each image.

A ship braving a wild sea.

A convoy crossing desert sands.

A long mountain rising up out of the desert.

Another man holding the ring and standing in a circular room.

A statue of a king, with a pedestal at his feet. Resting on it was the ring.

Elin couldn't help but feel like it was almost a hallway in some grand palace, instead of a tunnel in the bowels of an ancient mine.

They reached the archway at the end, and stepped into a large room.

It was circular. There were more carvings along these walls, along with several statues, as well. She sucked in a breath. It was just like the room inscribed on the tunnel wall.

There were five statues, each one made of gold. Kings and gods, if she had to guess. One looked Egyptian, a few weren't familiar, and one was a bearded, robed king.

God, these statues alone would be invaluable.

"This looks like Solomon," Hale said.

She strode across the room, stopping at the foot

of the statue. It was Solomon. Even carved in gold, he looked regal and wise. Flanking him, beautiful images were etched into the walls.

"That's his famous temple," Hale said, pointing to the picture on the left. "And that looks like the Ark of the Covenant sitting on the steps leading in."

Elin traced her fingers over another set of images on the right of the statue. "This is the well-known scene with the Queen of Sheba." A woman in a flowing dress had just swept into Solomon's court.

"His supposed lover?" Hale said.

"So the legends say."

But it was the stone pedestal in front of the statue that drew her attention.

She drew in a breath. Resting on the center of the pedestal was a chunky gold ring, with a golden star in the center, set with a large, uncut diamond.

It wasn't pretty. Elin circled the pedestal, taking in the ring from all angles. "Too big for a female's hand."

"But perfect for a king's," Hale said. "You think it really holds incredible knowledge?"

"No." Her hand hovered over the ring for a second, remembering the booby traps back in the shaft.

Taking a bracing breath, she gently picked the ring up.

No boulders rolled out of the wall, and no vats of molten lava poured over them. She shook her head at her fanciful thinking, and looked at the ring. It was surprisingly heavy, and she wondered if King Solomon had been the last person to wear it.

Suddenly, they heard noises. The scrape of stone, thumping, and the muffled sound of voices.

"Fuck," Hale snapped. "How did they find us?"

Elin stared back at the tunnel. It was the only way out. "We're cornered." Her gaze met his.

"We fight," he said.

She nodded. "Here." She shoved the ring at Hale. "Protect it." She then pulled out her stolen Beretta. There wasn't much ammunition left.

She saw the first Silk Road man enter the treasure room. She shifted to use one of the statues as cover, braced herself, and lifted the weapon. Out of the corner of her eye, she saw Hale step behind the statue of King Solomon, his big body tensed and waiting.

Elin took a shot and one man went down with a cry.

Others rushed in, and gunfire lit up the space.

Dammit, Elin wanted more time with Hale. She fired again, catching another man in the shoulder. More of Hale and his warmth, charm, and sexy body.

But as the Silk Road people rushed forward, Drift's shouts egging them on, she realized that they were trapped deep underground, with no way out. Their rescue would arrive soon...but they were going to be too late.

Her handgun clicked on empty. A big Silk Road man rushed at her and she threw the gun at him. The butt hit him in the face and he roared.

Another came at her, and she raised her hands. She swung to the side, landed a punch to the woman's gut, and spun away, bouncing on her feet.

Elin kept fighting, landing a solid kick to one man and a chop to another. She saw Hale charge forward. With several hard, mean moves, he took down two men. He had a tough, unforgiving style of hand-to-hand fighting.

More gunfire, and Elin ducked.

She saw Hale dive and roll across the floor. Damn, was he hit?

She landed a vicious front kick to a woman in front of her, fighting her way toward Hale. A punch slammed into her side, and she staggered back, half spinning.

Hale's startled shout reached her ears. *No.* She ducked low, and landed a hard, uppercut punch into a man's nose. Blood sprayed, and he rocked backward.

She spun. *Was Hale okay?*

Elin froze. Hale was...gone.

She searched the room. He wasn't where he'd been standing by the statue. He wasn't anywhere.

Another shot whizzed past her, and she dived to the floor. She crawled across the ground, heading toward where she'd last seen Hale. Where the hell had he gone?

Suddenly, two guards rushed at her. She kicked out at one and watched him tumble. She rolled up, getting ready to run.

A blow slammed into the back of her head.

Seeing stars, she staggered, landing on her

hands and knees. Someone grabbed her arms, wrenching them behind her back hard enough to hurt. She cried out.

John Drift stepped in front of her, his face set like stone. "Hello again, Agent Alexander."

Chapter Thirteen

Fuck. A trapdoor had opened up in the floor under Hale, and swallowed him.

He reached up, hammering at the rock above him with his fists. He couldn't see anything in the darkness, and he didn't have the flashlight, Elin did. The lantern was also in her backpack. *Double fuck.*

Now there was solid rock between him and her. She was stuck on the other side of it, with Silk Road trying to kill her. He roared in anger.

His chest tight, Hale slammed his palms against the rock. He felt all around, looking for a way to get it open and get back through.

He couldn't find anything, but he kept shoving and hitting until his knuckles tore and started to bleed. He *had* to get to her.

"Hold on, Elin." He felt around the other walls of the space he was in. It was a small tunnel. There had to be a way to trigger the trapdoor from this side. There had to be.

Finally, he slumped against the wall in defeat. *Nothing.* There was no way back to her.

Once again, he was stuck, unable to help

someone he cared about. He dragged in some deep breaths, each one hurting his chest. Was she okay? Did Drift have her?

Was she even still alive?

He had to find another way. He turned, facing the blackness. Keeping his fingers on the side wall, he moved down the tunnel, taking careful, shuffling steps.

Hale hadn't prayed in a very long time. Not since that long-ago mission where he'd lost the men he'd loved like brothers. He did now. He prayed Elin was still alive.

He reached an area where the tunnel split off in different directions. He stared into the blackness. Damn, he'd give anything for some light. Then he blinked. To the right, he could see a faint light at the end of the tunnel. He turned that way, and as the light got better, he picked up his pace.

He had no idea if he was moving farther away or closer to Elin.

Then, he heard something. He stilled and cocked his head. Running water.

He rounded a corner and ahead, he saw a large, round opening in the wall. Light was filtering in from narrow openings in the ceiling above. Water poured from the pipe, dropping into a long channel cut into the tunnel floor. The channel ran back into another dark, dank tunnel. Inside it, he heard the sound of something grinding and clanking.

What was that? He moved closer, peering into the darkness. He couldn't see whatever it was but his respect for the miners grew. There was some sort of machinery still active here.

Hale looked up. In his head, he tried to picture the layout of the mine, and the way they'd come. If his calculations were correct, this water was coming from the large pool above in the cavern, and there was some sort of plumbing system here pumping it back up to the waterfall. It had to be water-driven and he itched to examine it in detail. Whoever had built the mines had constructed one hell of a plumbing system.

He stared at the flowing water. If he could swim back up this tunnel, there was a chance he could make it all the way back into the pool in the cavern.

Back to Elin.

Hale kicked off his boots. He was a SEAL. The water was his terrain, and he'd been trained to hold his breath for a very long time.

He dumped his backpack and yanked it open. He'd only take what he needed. He tossed aside the sleeping bags and clothes. He kept his grappling gun. His fingers landed on some small silver balls in the bottom of the pack. Little prototype grenades he'd been playing with. He stuffed them in his pockets. Time for them to take a test run. He slipped the lighter backpack onto his back and tightened the straps.

Once again, he stared at the water-filled pipe ahead of him. He had no idea how wide it was farther up, and if he could even get through it. Hell, maybe it didn't even go back to the cavern pool.

Maybe he'd drown, trapped in King Solomon's Mines for eternity.

But saving Elin was a risk worth taking. It was one thing that Hale never regretted, going in to try and save his SEAL team. He hadn't thought it through or planned it well, but he hadn't hesitated to try and save them.

He sure as hell wasn't going to hesitate now.

Hale sucked in a few deep breaths, and then climbed into the rock-cut channel. The cool water hit his feet, and soaked the bottom of his trousers.

He sloshed through until he reached the circular pipe entrance. He pressed a knee to the edge, water hitting his face. He launched himself inside.

He pushed through the water, even as it tried to push him back. Soon he was swimming through the darkness, the light gone. He kept one hand on the wall to direct himself. The water flow pushed against him, but he kept his kicks strong and steady.

It was so fucking dark. He tried not to think about the walls closing in on him.

Hale's lungs started to burn, but he kept kicking with strong strokes. Elin would come for him. She was too driven and stubborn to give up. He wasn't going to fail her.

The tunnel curved, and Hale was pretty sure it was heading upward. *Come on.* God, maybe his oxygen-deprived brain was just playing games with him.

As dizziness hit him, he thought of Elin. Her smile, and the way it lit her eyes and warmed them. The way she kissed—with everything she had. The way she looked at him, like he was important.

He blinked. Light ahead. He blinked again, wondering if it was real or if he was imagining it.

He kept moving his legs, although he could feel each kick was losing strength. His lungs were burning, his brain screaming at him to open his mouth.

Suddenly, there was a shimmer of light coming from above. He looked up and saw a tunnel headed vertically up above him.

Clumsily, he kicked until he was moving up. Determination punched through him, and he dug deep for the last reserves of his strength. Near the top, his mouth opened reflexively, water flooding into him. Choking, he kicked again, and his head broke the surface.

Hale coughed the water out and then sucked in air. That's when he heard voices.

He slowly sank back into the water, just keeping his eyes above the surface. He worked to keep his breathing shallow and quiet, and slowly turned his head. He'd been right; he was back in the main cavern.

He spotted the Silk Road group entering the space. Two men were dragging a struggling Elin between them.

Everything in Hale wanted to leap up and charge out of the water, but he forced himself to stay still.

They shoved her onto a large rock and he saw

that her hands were tied behind her back. He also saw that one side of her face was swelling, with bruises forming.

Bastards. Hale's hands curled into fists. Someone would pay.

John Drift stepped forward, eyeing Elin like she was some specimen for him to dissect.

"How did you find us?" she demanded.

"Claude liked pretty gadgets in all his toys. Your vehicle was outfitted with a tracker."

Hale cursed inwardly. They should have known. It explained why Drift hadn't chased after them in the helicopter when they'd first gotten away.

"Where is the Seal of Solomon?" the man said.

Hale jerked. Hell, he'd completely forgotten about the damn ring. He touched his pocket and felt the slight bulge.

"I don't know," Elin answered. "We didn't find it."

Drift's gaze narrowed. "I saw the paintings, Agent Alexander. The one showing the ring at the foot of the statue of King Solomon. Right where we found you."

"It wasn't there."

Drift nodded. A guard stepped forward and punched Elin in the gut. She doubled over with a groan.

Hale had to hold himself back. It was one of the hardest things he'd ever done. He bit down hard on his lip, instead.

The last time he'd rushed in, unprepared, and it had cost his fellow SEALs their lives.

"Where is Solomon's ring?" Drift asked again.

"I don't know. There is no other way to say it."

Drift moved fast and slapped her across the face. Her lip split, bleeding.

Hale stayed on the deeper side of the pool and moved to the rocky edge, trying to calm his racing heart. *Don't go in halfcocked. You've done that before.*

Elin's life depended on him.

Think, Hale. He tried to remind himself that she was trained, that she could handle this. He knew Elin Alexander was the last person who needed him to run in like an action hero.

What she really needed was for him to think. He studied the group. Four guards and Drift. Of course, they were all armed and he wasn't...but that didn't mean he was helpless. That was doable. Hale could take them.

The closest guard to Hale was partly hidden from the others by a rock pillar and standing right beside the water. *Target Number One acquired.*

Slowly, inch by inch, Hale climbed out of the pool. He slipped into combat mode as easily as breathing. His vitals steadied and his concentration was centered on his target, even as he monitored the rest of the room.

He blocked the sounds of flesh hitting flesh, and Elin's harsh expulsion of air. Whoever had hit her would regret it shortly.

Hale moved silently, and then grabbed the man from behind, slamming a hand over the guard's mouth. Hale dragged the man backward into the water. He jerked the man down, and just as the guard overcame his surprise, Hale quickly twisted the man's neck. There was a muffled crack, and his body sank down into the water.

Hale grabbed for him, thinking he'd check for a weapon. But the body slipped into deep water and Hale cursed.

Stick to the plan. One down, four to go.

Hale climbed out of the water and crouched behind a rock. Suddenly, he heard Elin scream. The sound was like claws to his soul.

"I love this knife." Drift's voice. "It's even prettier coated in your blood, Special Agent Alexander."

Hale gritted his teeth, even as his head snapped up. His thoughts coalesced into one direction. Save Elin.

He slipped his backpack off his shoulders and yanked out his grappling gun. Peering around the pillar, he took in the locations of the others.

Take one out with the grappling gun and attack the next one closest to him. It would leave Elin open to Drift and the final guard. Damn, it was a huge risk.

"Enough of this." Drift pulled out his gun and aimed it directly at Elin's chest.

No. A red haze covered Hale's vision. For a second, he saw the insurgents killing his SEAL commander, Sean, then the others, one by one.

He couldn't lose Elin. Hale lifted the grappling gun and aimed at the nearest guard.

He fired. He heard the distinctive sound it made

as the bolt and rope flew across the space. He charged toward the other guard, and saw the grappling hook slam into the guard's chest with a spray of blood.

Two down. Three to go.

"What the fuck?" someone yelled.

Hale tackled his next target, and landed a hard blow to the man's head, knocking him unconscious. He spied a knife in the man's slackened hand and snatched it up, already springing away.

Three down. Two to go.

Gunfire echoed in the cavern, bullets peppering the ground where he'd been standing.

Hale dived, sliding across the rocky ground on his side. He spun, sighted his next target, and threw the knife.

It nailed the man in the shoulder, shock and pain skittering across his broad face. He staggered backward and Hale leaped up. He landed on the man and drove him to the ground. The man's head connected with the ground with a dull thud.

Four down. One to go.

Hale yanked out the knife, jumped up, and spun.

His chest constricted. Elin had somehow freed her hands and was wrestling with Drift for control of the gun. He started forward, his hand tightening on the bloody hilt of the knife.

Elin and Drift strained, turning in an untidy circle. Drift was stronger and managed to turn the gun to aim it at the center of Elin's chest.

The gun went off.

Elin! No!

Hale sprinted forward, rushing forward as Elin's body fell backward and hit the ground. Drift had disappeared.

Hale dropped heavily to his knees. She was flat on her back, her face twisted in pain. There was a ragged hole in the center of her khaki shirt.

He slid an arm beneath her. "Elin." His voice was choked.

No one could survive a shot like this.

"Hale," she croaked out, her hand groping for his.

He grabbed it, squeezing her fingers tight. "God, baby."

"I…" Her voice broke off, her body going lax and her eyes drifting closed.

"No." A hollow feeling burst inside him. She was so warm, but he knew it would fade. Hale felt like his insides had been shredded. He'd failed her. He'd been too late.

"Get the secondary team in here!" Drift's shout came from the other side of the cavern. "Get them in here. The woman's dead, but I want Carter contained, and I want the ring!"

The sounds of running footsteps and shouts penetrated the ice encasing Hale. He fought through his shock and pain. Drift had more people coming.

They weren't going to touch Elin again.

He scooped her into his arms, spun, and waded back into the pool.

He was getting her far away from fucking Drift and Silk Road. He dived down into the water, swimming for the tunnel he'd come up through. He held Elin tight against his chest and tried not to think. Tried not to think about the fact that he'd lost her. Lost the woman he was falling in love with.

Suddenly, she started moving in his arms, thrashing against him.

Shit, she was still alive. He felt like a light burst inside him. She was trying to breathe.

He lifted her up to his face and pressed his mouth to hers. He breathed into her, and then pulled back and kicked as fast and hard as he could.

It felt like forever, but finally they whooshed out of the pipe and into the rock-cut channel with a splash.

Elin was gagging and coughing up water. Hale managed to climb over the side of the channel with her, and collapsed on the ground. He spun her around, his hands shaking, and pushed her sodden hair out of her face.

"Elin?"

She coughed again and pressed a hand to her chest. "Dammit. What were you trying to do, drown me?"

"Drift shot you point-blank in the chest. I thought you were *dead*." Hale's voice cracked on the last word.

Elin stilled, her wide eyes meeting his. She reached forward, dropped her head to his chest and hugged him hard. He wrapped his arms around her and held on tight, absorbing the fact that she was breathing and alive in his arms.

She pulled back slowly, her hand caressing his jaw. "I'm alive because of you. Or because of your shirt."

She lifted up the hem of her khaki shirt, and Hale saw the T-shirt she'd borrowed. He hadn't noticed before, but it was his experimental, anti-ballistic shirt.

The fabric was deformed right in the center, where it had stopped the bullet.

Jesus. He pushed it up. "I hadn't finished testing it. It's made from a structured polymer composite, and it worked in the lab, but still hasn't passed field testing."

"I like when you talk geek," she said. "The shirt works."

"That still had to hurt." He gently touched her stomach.

"Yeah. It was like getting hit with a sledgehammer. I must have passed out, and it winded me."

He cupped her cheeks. "Winded now?"

She licked her lips. "No."

He pulled her forward and kissed her. "Elin. I...think I'm fucking falling in love with you."

She stared at him, her mouth dropping open.

He shot her a rueful smile. "Wow, Agent Alexander has nothing to say."

Her hands gripped his wrists. "I just got shot, Carter. Give me a second." She cupped his cheek. "I really suck at this love thing."

"Well, I can't say I have much experience with it, either."

"Our odds of success suck."

He grinned at her. "I happen to like long odds."

She smiled back. "Me, too. But right now, we have a mission to finish, and some bad guys to catch."

Hale's gaze drifted to her battered face. "I'm pretty eager to get my hands on Drift."

"You can't kill him," she warned. "I'm law enforcement, remember?"

Hale pulled her to her feet. "I know a lot of ways to hurt him without killing him."

Chapter Fourteen

Elin kicked beside Hale as they swam back up into the pool. Without his strength and power in the water, she would never have made it.

They surfaced near the waterfall, and she took some deep breaths. Hale pressed a finger to his lips and she nodded. They swam toward the edge of the pool. The cavern was eerily quiet.

They had no weapons, except for the small, sphere-shaped grenades he'd given her. The metallic balls were heavy in her pocket, and Hale had said he'd developed them himself. Besides, she had a former Navy SEAL with her. He was pretty deadly, too.

And he was hers.

Elin stumbled a little pulling herself out of the water before she righted herself. Oh, that knowledge excited her and left her dry-mouthed. She still had scars on her heart from her failed marriage, and her feelings for Hale had bloomed fast, in the middle of a dangerous mission they still hadn't finished.

But she knew this was the real deal. Knew it deep in her bones. She also knew he'd never hurt her. Hell, he'd almost gotten killed rescuing her.

It was herself she didn't trust. Elin had promised to love Matthew and he'd promised to love her—but it hadn't lasted. She knew they were both to blame, that they'd both given up somewhere along the line.

She shook her head. She needed to focus on getting Drift and staying alive. On keeping herself and Hale alive. She could obsess over whatever this was with Hale later.

They crept across the cavern. Where the hell was Drift? Hale had his head tilted, and then he pointed to the far side of the cavern.

A hidden rock door that she and Hale hadn't discovered earlier was wedged open. God, it looked like someone had taken a jackhammer to it. The slab of rock was cracked, and propped open with a large rock. They hurried over and, as they crossed the space, Hale knelt down and picked up a large rock. She watched him settle it in his hand. In his other hand, he held two metallic grenades.

"You have your grenades?" he murmured.

She fished them out.

"The silver one is a smoke bomb," he told her. "The black one is a magnetic bomb."

"You're a handy guy to have around, Carter." She ran the balls through her fingers.

He gripped her hand, squeezed. "Don't forget that."

They paused at the propped-open doorway, and she heard the echo of voices inside.

"Search every tunnel, if you have to," Drift ordered. "Carter has the ring. I'm sure of it."

Elin pointed inside and Hale nodded. She peered around the edge.

Inside was a large, rectangular room with rough rock walls. It was lined on each side with what looked like stone bathtubs hewn out of rock.

"Looks like it was a smelting room." Hale's voice was a deep whisper.

A place where the ancient miners had smelted their gold and turned it into bars. The Silk Road team was clustered in the center of the space. Elin glanced up and spotted some rotted timbers attached to the roof. Maybe the remnants of some sort of old type of crane.

She looked back at Hale and he nodded.

Elin set her shoulders back and pulled out the small balls. She tossed them, aiming for the group. She heard the quiet rattle as they rolled across the ground. Some of the men were turning, frowning at the sound.

The magnetic grenade exploded first, strips of highly magnetized metal bursting out.

The men closest to the grenade jerked as they

were tugged in by the strong magnet. Belts, weapons, and anything else metallic stuck to the grenade. The men all cursed and struggled, landing in a tangle of limbs.

Elin smiled. She'd never seen anything like it and she wanted more of those little grenades.

Then, the smoke grenade went off with a *bang*.

Smoke filled the room, and the Silk Road guards started shouting. Elin and Hale rushed in.

She moved to the left, taking one man down with a hard chop between his shoulder blades. A knife fell from his hand and clattered to the ground.

Nice. She snatched it up and jumped over him. She looked up to see a woman stumble out of the smoke. Elin kicked the woman in the gut, sending her flying.

"Elin!"

Hale's cry made her spin. Another attacker, a mountain of a man with a shaved head, charged out of the smoke. He had an assault rifle aimed at her.

She ducked. Bullets sprayed above her head, and she heard something crash. A second later, Hale swept past her. He slammed his rock into the man's head. The man made a strangled groan and collapsed.

Elin rose, just as another man rushed out of the smoke at her. He was also a big bruiser, and he held a combat knife easily in his right hand.

"Come on, then." She held her knife up. She had trained with a fellow agent who specialized in knife fighting.

They circled each other, an edgy smile on the big guy's face. Clearly, he thought he could take her down easily.

Go ahead, asshole. Underestimate me. He darted in and Elin spun. She saw him frown, surprised she wasn't where he expected her to be. She came in low, sliced her blade against his arm, and opened up his bicep.

With a pained shout, he leaped back, slapping his other hand over the bleeding cut.

Elin smiled.

With a roar, the man rushed at her. She didn't dodge or duck. She jumped straight at him, surprising him yet again.

His knife moved past her and her knees hit his chest. She stabbed her knife into his shoulder. Once, twice. He was already falling when she leaped off him.

That's when she heard Hale's harsh grunt. She swiveled.

Her gut cramped. A Silk Road man was behind Hale, a garrote wire around Hale's throat. The man was pulling hard, and Hale tugged at the wire, his face twisted with strain.

He fell to his knees, and Elin raced toward them.

***

"I'm gonna mess you up, pretty boy."

The Silk Road man leaned in close behind Hale. The bastard was strong. As the man kept trash-talking in Hale's ear, he focused on keeping the wire off his throat.

Hale had a finger up under it and it was biting into his skin. Blood slid down his hand and arm.

"Once you're good and bleeding, then I'll make you watch while I hurt your woman."

The insurgents had done that to Hale. Made him watch while they'd tortured his friends. He'd watched them all die, one by one.

His breathing turned harsh, his mind whirled. Suddenly, he was in a different desert, deep voices speaking Arabic all around him.

God, he was going to die here just like his friends.

"Hale!"

The feminine shout broke him out of his overpowering memories. His eyes snapped open. He saw a knife land in front of him, scraping on the rock before it hit his knee.

Elin's voice. *Elin.*

Energy flooded him. The woman he loved was here, fighting for her life, fighting for him. He'd escaped that long-ago hellhole. He'd survived.

And since then, he'd dishonored his team mates by living a half life. It was time to fucking change that.

Hale threw his head back. The back of his skull cracked against his captor's nose, and the man howled.

The garrote wire loosened a little and Hale

quickly pushed forward. He reached down, his fingers brushing the knife.

Suddenly, the wire pulled tight again, cutting into his skin. *Fuck.*

Hale couldn't breathe. He looked up and saw Elin fighting with another guard. *Fuck this.* He pushed forward, letting the wire sink into his skin. He felt the slide of warm blood down his neck.

His fingers brushed rock, then metal. He grabbed the knife, clutched the hilt, then rammed it back behind him.

His attacker grunted. The wire fell away.

Sucking in air, Hale spun on his knees and buried the knife in the man's gut. A few short, well aimed stabs, and the man fell back, clutching his bleeding stomach.

Hale leaped up and sprinted toward Elin.

He skidded to a halt. Her attacker was down. She was standing there, chest heaving, calmly taking the man's rifle.

She was fucking magnificent. And all his.

Suddenly Drift appeared from the dissipating smoke, a gun aimed right at Elin's back.

No! Hale shoved his hand in his pocket and grabbed the Seal of Solomon.

"Drift!" Hale tossed the ring.

Drift turned and saw the ring. He dodged away from Elin and leaped to catch the ancient artifact.

Then Hale heard something else that made his blood run cold. A buzzing sound echoing off the rock walls.

Elin's head snapped up, her eyes widening.

The drone shot out of a nearby tunnel. It was identical to the one that had attacked them at the outpost.

Gunfire sprayed the room.

Elin took three running steps and dived into Hale. They slammed together, hitting the ground. Hale rolled them behind one of the stone tubs, just as more gunfire peppered the rock all around them.

***

Elin couldn't see a way out. The drone swiveled, still firing. Her hands tightened on her stolen rifle and she watched bullets send the few remaining Silk Road team members scattering.

"We can use these tubs for cover," Hale said, "and make our way toward the exit."

She eyed the long line of stone tubs. They gave solid cover, but when they ran between them, they'd be out in the open.

More gunfire had them both ducking.

"Come on." Hale grabbed her hand and tugged her up.

They sprinted as fast as they could and dived in behind the next tub. Bullets slammed into the ground nearby, flecks of rock pinging at their skin.

They both dropped down to the floor and Hale covered her with his body. She tried to elbow him off, but the big, overprotective hero wouldn't budge.

More bullets rained down around them. They were pinned down.

Hale lifted his head and cursed. "Dammit."

Elin followed his gaze and saw Drift across the room, hiding behind another tub. He had the Seal of Solomon in his hand.

And he was only two tubs away from getting to the exit.

"No fucking way." Hale crouched, every muscle in his body tense. "That bastard is *not* getting out of here—"

"Hale! It's too dangerous."

He gripped her chin. "He hurt you. He tried to kill you." Hale pressed a bruising kiss to her lips and then leaped over the tub.

Her heart jumped into her throat. She turned and watched as he ran like a football player—zig zagging across the room. He shoved one Silk Road man out of the way, then dived and slammed into Drift. The two of them rolled across the floor, each wrestling to get on top of the other.

The drone swiveled, opening fire in their direction.

No, you don't. Elin jumped up and scrambled over to one of the downed bodies. She swung the rifle up and dropped down on one knee. She didn't bother aiming. She just wanted to cause a distraction and give Hale some cover fire.

Hale and Drift rolled out from behind the tub, out in the open. The drone started turning.

Right now, Elin didn't care about the ring or the mission or her job. She just wanted to get Hale and herself out of there alive.

She fired at the drone. Her first shots missed and she swallowed back her threatening panic. She fired again and this time, one of her shots hit it. She watched it wobble. Yes! She'd hit something vital. It lowered to the ground and Elin grinned.

But as its guns moved, she realized that while she'd stopped it flying, she hadn't damaged its weapons. It opened fire.

Bullets hit near Hale and Drift. Hale's body jerked.

"No!" Elin aimed again and fired at the drone.

Hale fell backward and Drift rose up, a smile on his face.

Her gun clicked empty. *Screw this.* She tossed the rifle and leaped over a tub, running fast. She flew at Drift, jumping into a roundhouse kick. Her boot slammed into the man's jaw. The ring flew from his hand, hit the ground with a ping, and rolled away.

She raced over to Hale. "Move." The left leg of his cargo pants was soaked with blood and she stomped back her panic. *Please don't have hit something vital.* Slinging an arm around his back, she tried to move him. "Cover. Now."

He was trying to move, but he couldn't get his injured leg under him. And he was so damn heavy.

She grunted, tugging on him. The closest tub looked like it was miles away.

With a sudden roar, John Drift leaped at them. "The ring is mine!"

In a split second, Elin let go of Hale and braced for Drift's weight. As he hit her, she used the momentum to swing him around.

The drone opened fire and Elin held Drift up like

a human shield in front of her and Hale.

The actor's body shuddered under the bullets hitting his back. He stared at Elin, his mouth open in shock and his eyes wide.

"Mine," he choked out.

"No, asshole, mine. And you're over."

Blood dribbled out of his mouth. She shoved him away and spun back to Hale.

"Come on." She slid an arm around him. "Let's move."

Elin heard a mechanical whirr. Dread sliding down her spine, she looked over her shoulder and saw the drone was back in the air, but only a foot off the ground. It wasn't stable, bobbing like crazy.

But as she watched, its guns swiveled and aimed right at them.

Time slowed down, and she tightened her hold around Hale. They were trapped, several feet away from cover, and directly in the line of fire.

Chapter Fifteen

Fighting through the pain, Hale watched the drone aim straight at them.

Using the last of his strength, he pushed himself up. He knocked Elin to the ground and flung himself on top of her. He curled his body around her.

"Hale." Her fingers dug into him, her body shoving against him. "It'll shoot you!"

"I know." But she'd hopefully be safe. "You promise me you'll get out of here, and you'll live. Get that fancy promotion and go climb the Eiffel Tower. For both of us."

Her face went pale. "Hale."

Emotion stormed through him. This woman clicked with him. Like a piece of the puzzle he hadn't known was missing all his life.

"Baby." He pressed his forehead to hers. Behind them, he heard the whirr of the drone reloading. "I love you."

Elin made a choked sound, her fingers pressing against his cheek.

Then the roar of gunfire filled the room.

Hale squeezed his eyes closed and waited for the bullets to rip into him.

But nothing happened.

Instead, voices shouting and more shots on the other side of the room filled his ears. He lifted his head. Several people wearing black tactical vests were running in from the cavern entrance.

The drone swiveled to face this new threat.

"Stop!" A man's deep voice echoed through the room.

Hale blinked and saw that it was Declan. He had his MP4 aimed at the drone. Flanking him were Coop, Morgan, and Cal.

Dec pointed at Hale and Elin. "She's FBI. He's mine. Treasure Hunter Security. They were undercover."

Lights blinked on the drone and a hush filled the room. The only sounds were the local agents moving to subdue the remaining Silk Road men.

"Stand down, or I will hunt you down and make you fucking regret ever putting my people at risk." Dec's voice had turned hard and cold.

The drone's weapons retracted.

"Hale!" Coop and Morgan dropped down beside Hale and Elin.

Elin shoved at him, rolling him off her. Pain exploded in his leg and he groaned.

"He's been shot." She urged him to lie back on the ground, her hands touching his blood-soaked thigh. "There's a lot of blood."

Hale blinked. Was that panic in her normally-controlled voice?

"Bullet might have nicked an artery." She tore the fabric of his pants.

He reached out and grabbed her hand. "Elin?" She ignored him, her fingers pressing to his skin. "Babe, it's a flesh wound."

"I know you pretty well by now, Carter," she said. "You could be bleeding to death and still say it's just a flesh wound."

Morgan snorted. "She has you pegged, Hale."

"Let me see?" Dec shouldered forward, nudging Elin back. His hands touched Hale's thigh wound with quick, practiced moves. Dec sat back. "It looks like a flesh wound."

"There's so much blood," Elin said. "He couldn't stand before."

"Winded," Hale said. "That bastard Drift got a good hit in."

Dec looked over his shoulder. "Someone get over here with the first aid kit."

Soon, a NIA agent dropped down beside them with a small kit. The man set to work.

"She needs checking, too," Hale said. "She has an injury on her hand and she was beaten pretty badly earlier."

"I'm fine."

They stared at each other.

Dec eyed Hale and Elin. "You guys look like you've been through hell."

"You could say that." As the medic cleaned Hale's wound with antiseptic, Hale winced at the sting.

Dec touched his ear. "Message from Burke. He says good job, glad you're both okay, and did you find the ring?"

Elin gasped. She ran a hand through her hair and looked dazed. "Ah, I forgot about the ring. Drift had it. I saw him drop it in the fight, but…"

The faintest smile tilted Dec's lips. "You were more concerned about someone else?"

Elin lifted her chin. "Yes."

Hale smiled and held up his hand. "Here you go."

Everybody gasped. He was holding the Seal of Solomon that he'd managed to scoop up off the ground in the fight with Drift. He urged Elin to take it, and she gingerly took the ring. Then she turned and handed it to Dec.

Dec pulled out a slim-line tablet and turned it over. Agent Alastair Burke's face filled the screen. "Well done, Elin. You too, Hale."

"Let me see them." Darcy's aggravated voice.

"Wait—" Burke said.

"No." Darcy elbowed Burke out of the way, and appeared on the screen. "Is everyone okay?"

"We're okay, Darce," Hale answered.

She blew out a breath. "Thank God."

"You want to get out of my lap?" Burke said dryly.

Spots of color appeared on Darcy's cheeks. "Take care of yourselves and I'll see you when you get home."

Burke reappeared.

"We were nearly killed by that fucking drone," Hale bit out. "Twice. Is that some FBI toy?"

"No." Burke's tone turned stone hard. "It's someone else's toy. They didn't know that you two were undercover. They thought you were Silk Road."

Suddenly, Dec stiffened. "It belongs to the fucking team in black that we crossed paths with in Madagascar."

"Let it go," Burke said. "Turn me toward the drone."

Dec did as ordered, grumbling as he did.

"Deactivate," Burke said.

Nothing happened. The drone still hovered unsteadily, watching them.

"You see the ring Ward is holding? The Seal of Solomon. You want it, then deactivate your fucking drone. You can make a damn appointment with my office, if you want the ring and your drone."

A second later, the drone powered down and lowered to the ground. Several agents hurried over to secure it. Dec swiveled the tablet again.

Burke looked at Elin. "Really great work, Elin. Looks like you secured yourself that promotion you were after. I'm putting you forward for the Interpol team. Hope you like France."

She blinked. "Thank you."

Hearing the words made Hale's chest spasm. Her dream. Everything she'd been working toward and hoping for. Her chance to find justice for her father.

As the medic finished patching up his leg, Hale closed his eyes.

Elin deserved this promotion. She deserved to have everything she loved. And while he'd told her how he felt, she hadn't said she loved him back.

***

Once the medic had finished checking her over, Elin walked with the NIA and Namibian CIS agents. She was going to be sore for a while, and have some spectacular bruises, but nothing was broken.

She focused on finalizing the details for the detainment and arrests of the Silk Road people still alive. There was also work to be done with the Namibian government to secure the mine.

But, to be honest, those were the last things she really cared about right now.

She glanced back to where Ronin and Cal had their arms around Hale. He was moving pretty well, and looked much better, now that he'd been patched up.

He hadn't looked at her once.

She swallowed. Maybe reality was setting in. Maybe his confession of love was just because of their dire circumstances. Hell, all of this between them had happened so fast and had been fueled by adrenaline. She knew situations like this could make people do and say crazy things.

They'd made a hell of a team...but maybe he was feeling differently now.

Tired, sore, and running on fumes, Elin moved on autopilot as they wound back through the tunnels, and used the platform and ropes the THS team had rigged up in the main shaft.

When she stepped out into the sunshine, she

blinked. She had no idea what time of day it was, and had, for some reason, been expecting darkness.

Down the hill, she spotted a convoy of beige SUVs, all covered in desert dust. Nearby, was Drift's black helicopter, and another one that she guessed the THS team had arrived in.

One of the lead agents shook hands with Declan. "Thanks for your help."

Dec nodded. "My team and I will take the helicopters out, and secure the Seal of Solomon as Agent Burke organized."

"And we'll take these men into custody and secure the site," the agent said, his teeth very white against his dark skin. He turned to look at Elin. "We've been instructed to give you a ride, Agent Alexander. Agent Burke suggested you'd want to oversee charging the Silk Road members."

She looked at the convoy, and a rock lodged in her chest. She'd be traveling with the agents, and Hale would be flying away in the helicopter.

"Hey." Hale stepped in front of her, his handsome face serious.

Elin felt something tremble deep inside her. His gaze was on her, but she couldn't read what he was thinking...or feeling.

"Hey," she replied quietly.

"I wanted to thank you."

She blinked. *Thank her?*

"You're a hell of an agent, Elin. The best I've worked with. Hell, you could've been a SEAL."

"We work well together."

"I know I said some things down there..." His

voice trailed off.

She waited, her chest tight.

He cleared his throat and took a deep breath. "Congratulations on the promotion. I don't know of anyone who deserves it more."

Promotion? She sucked in a breath. He thought she was thinking about the damn promotion? Pain was a sharp, spiky ball inside her. She couldn't seem to find the words she needed. The only thing she could think was that maybe he was using this as a way out.

In the light of day, Hale had realized that he wasn't in love with her. The Hale Carter she knew was a fighter who never gave up, so if he really wanted her, he'd tell her.

He reached out and tucked a strand of hair back behind her ear. "You take care of yourself. You deserve to follow your dreams. When you climb the Eiffel Tower, think of me."

Then he turned, and limped toward the helicopter.

Just like that. Elin pressed her lips together, breathing through the pain clawing at her. It appeared that she was very easy for men to walk away from.

***

Every step away from her hurt.

Hale knew he was doing the right thing. Elin deserved to be happy, and if he confessed everything he felt for her... If he told her how much he wanted her, then he'd be dragging her away from her dream.

She was damn good at her job, and he wouldn't get in the way of what she wanted. Besides, he didn't have much to offer her except life with a burned-out, former SEAL with commitment issues of his own—

A hand grabbed his arm and spun him around.

"Just like that?" Elin's voice was sharp as a blade.

"What?" He frowned at her.

"We go through hell together, have each other's backs, we fight side by side—" Her face was incandescent with rage.

"Elin—"

Her blue eyes glittered. "We saved each other's lives, fucked each other's brains out—"

"Ooh." Morgan's amused voice from nearby.

Hale was conscious of everyone staring at them, but he only had eyes for Elin.

"You told me you were falling in love with me." She thrust her hands on her hips. "Was that just one of your lines, Carter?"

"No!"

"You're walking away!" Her voice lowered. "All you have to say is 'take care of yourself, Elin'?"

Something hot flooded through him. "You were outstanding on this mission. Brilliant. You're born for this kind of work. You left your marriage for this job, for a chance to right the wrong against your parents. And now you're set to get an amazing promotion you deserve. I won't ruin it for you!"

There was rapt silence around them and he felt everyone's attention like a solid thing.

Elin took a step closer and jabbed a finger in his chest. "I had a man say he loved me once, and he had no trouble walking away." Bitterness filled her voice. "Guess I'm extra lucky to have it happen a second time."

Hale narrowed his eyes. She couldn't be serious? She turned to walk away but this time he grabbed her arms. He yanked her in close and she collided with his chest. He wrapped his arms around her, dragging her up onto her toes.

"Do not compare me to that asshole."

"You're walking away." Tears gleamed in her eyes. She looked down, making an angry sound, and tried to pull away from him.

He didn't let her move. "Baby." He cupped her face with one hand.

"If you don't love me, just leave."

"I was wrong in the mine," he said. "About falling in love with you."

She jerked like he'd shot her. God, he was an idiot. He hurried on. "Because I'm not falling in love with you. I already love you."

She went still now, and raised her gaze. He saw a flash of something soft and hopeful in her face.

"I love you, Elin. So much that I want you to be happy, and do what makes you happy."

Her hands fisted in his shirt. "Ask me what makes me happy, Hale."

"I saw you down there with the bad guys, baby. I can see for myself."

She straightened. "Ask me."

Suddenly, Hale felt like he was standing on the edge of a very big cliff, the ground crumbling away under his feet.

"What makes you happy, Elin?" he asked quietly.

"You. The man I love. The man who came for me. The man who threw himself over me to protect me. The man who makes me smile, who is sexy as hell, who makes my mind go blank whenever he smiles at me, or when he touches me."

God. "Elin."

He took her mouth with his, kissing her deep. She tasted like Elin and her hands gripped him hard. Hale took every advantage, pulling her closer and kissing her harder. So she'd never, ever doubt how he felt about her.

Then he heard clapping and cheering around them. Hale reluctantly lifted his head, holding Elin tight. Dec was smiling and shaking his head.

"Hale Carter takes the fall." Morgan came up and slapped a hand against Hale's back. "Never thought I'd see the day."

"Nice work, buddy." Coop watched them with a small smile.

From beside Dec, Cal gave Hale a thumbs-up.

"I'll find work in France," Hale told Elin. "I'm sure there are security firms who'd take me and—"

She smiled at him. "Well, I hear they have the FBI in Denver, too. And the Eiffel Tower isn't going anywhere."

He took her mouth with his and kissed her
again.

Chapter Sixteen

Ronin Cooper watched the beautiful bride walk down the aisle.

She wore a simple V-necked ivory gown that skimmed slim curves, her dark hair was pulled up in an elegant twist, and her face was radiant. She stared down the red carpet at her groom.

Ronin looked at Dec waiting for his bride.

The man looked happy. Really happy.

Dec and Layne were getting married on the lawn just outside the Denver Museum of Nature and Science at City Park. White chairs had been set out, and the backdrop for the ceremony was a perfect view of the Denver city skyline and the magnificent Rocky Mountains.

But the bride and groom only had eyes for each other.

In the Denver sunlight, Ronin sat beside Sydney. Logan was standing up with Dec as best man. They watched their friends exchange their vows and pledge their lives to each other.

He'd known Dec a long time, and knew the man had come home with scars. Dark scars. Ronin's hand curled into a fist on his knee. Dec was one of the lucky ones, who'd found a way out of the darkness, and into the arms of a smart, sexy woman who loved him completely.

Ronin knew there was no light for him.

Later, he found himself surrounded by his THS friends at the reception inside the museum. Everyone was laughing and drinking. Morgan's killer legs were on display in her short dress, and she was leaning against Zach. The man was keeping a tight arm around his woman, smiling down at her.

Ronin lifted his beer and took a sip. Layne, Dani, and Sydney were on the dance floor, shimmying to the music. Dec, Logan, and Cal were standing nearby, scowling at any men who dared get too close to their women. Professor Ward and Penelope Ward were dancing together, the tiny woman leaning into her husband. They moved smoothly across the floor, putting most of the younger couples to shame. They moved in a way that showed the years they'd had together.

Hale's deep laugh drew Ronin's gaze back to the table. Across from him, Elin and Hale were sitting side-by-side, gazing at each other. They looked like they were the only two people in the room. Ronin could hardly believe that Hale had gone and fallen in love with an FBI agent. But they looked right. They clicked.

Suddenly, Darcy dropped down beside Ronin and snatched up a glass of champagne. Her glossy hair swung as she tilted the glass back and she looked as polished as ever in her aquamarine bridesmaid gown. "Having fun?" she said.

Ronin just grunted.

"I know that's Ronin-speak for you're just waiting for the right time to find a dark shadow you can slip away into," she said.

"Weddings aren't really my thing."

"Right, and with all these loved-up couples around, it makes you feel like a third wheel?" She wrinkled her nose.

"Something like that." He was just hoping it wasn't contagious.

"You look mighty fine in your suit." She sipped her champagne. "I can't believe Sydney got Logan in a suit. And it looks like he had a haircut."

"She promised him sexual favors."

Darcy snorted. "Figures." Her gaze fell on Elin and Hale across the table. "Sounds like Elin is settling well into Denver. God, they had a spectacular argument about whether they were moving to Lyon in France or Denver, right in the middle of the office." Darcy shook her head. "I was ready to start taking bets. Anyway, she convinced Hale she wanted to stay stateside, and not run off after something that was in the past. She wanted something real, and she wanted them to make a home." Darcy sighed. "Hale's planning to teach her to snowboard in the winter."

"The man is a machine on the snow."

"You aren't too shabby yourself," Darcy said. Then she sniffed. "Me, I prefer a hot drink by the fireplace in the lodge."

He smiled. Darcy did like her creature comforts. "So, any jobs on the horizon?"

"There's always something. We've got one coming up doing some security with Zach right here at the museum. Some new exhibit."

Ronin didn't love museum security work. It was generally slow and uneventful. He liked action, and preferred to be in the field. He didn't like to stop in one place for too long. If you did that, the past could catch up to you.

He looked up to see Darcy's far-too-perceptive blue-gray gaze on him. "Do you miss the SEALs?"

His hands clenched on his beer bottle. "No."

"The CIA?"

"No."

She sighed. "I know that's macho man speak for you don't want to talk about it."

"You're a smart lady, Darcy Ward." Around them, their friends were laughing, and Ronin tried to relax. The past was the past. He knew it was possible to escape it, he'd seen the way the dark shadows in Hale's eyes were slowly melting away, and in Declan's today. But Ronin's shadows were etched in his bones, in his soul. His were going nowhere.

Dec appeared. "Quit flirting with my sister."

Darcy made a scoffing sound. "All the men you hire end up being like brothers to me, Dec." Then she stiffened, her gaze on the other side of the room. "I *cannot* believe you invited Agent Arrogant and Annoying to your wedding, Dec." Her tone was disgruntled.

"My wedding, so I get to invite whoever I like," Dec said.

Ronin did his best to hide his amusement and spotted a suit-clad Agent Burke chatting with Zach and Morgan.

Darcy made a huffing sound. "I don't know how anyone could be friends with that man." Her eyes widened and she hissed. "He's coming this way. He was threatening to corner me for a *dance*." She turned and disappeared into the crowd.

Dec was looking at Burke. "Poor guy's been dealing with the media frenzy about the famous John Drift turning out to be a murdering antiquities thief."

Everyone was very interested in how John Drift had died in an ancient mine in the middle of the Kalahari Desert. Thankfully, Burke had been keeping most of the details out of the press.

"He tell you what he did with the Seal of Solomon?" Ronin asked.

"Nope." Dec took a sip of his drink. "And I didn't ask."

Layne arrived in a cloud of pretty perfume. "I fancy a dance with my new husband."

Dec groaned, but Ronin saw the light in his eyes. The man would do anything for his woman.

After Layne had coaxed Dec onto the dance floor, Ronin continued to sip his beer. It felt good to be around his friends, to absorb some of their happiness. Maybe a little bit of it would rub off on him.

A flash of color near the bar caught his eye. A woman was watching him.

She was sitting on a stool, deep in the shadows,

and her red hair glinted in the low light. No, not red. More of a deep copper.

Instincts flaring, Ronin set his beer down and stood. The way she was watching their group wasn't casual. It was sharp, and far too interested.

As soon as she noticed that he was watching her, she stood. Their gazes clashed for a second across the crowded room. Blunt bangs fell almost to eyes that were too far away for him to see their color.

Then she spun and slipped away.

She was heading toward the restrooms. Ronin picked up speed, dodging around people. He'd honed his instincts over his various careers, and right now they were telling him something wasn't right.

He reached the restrooms, but the hall was empty. He slammed into the women's restroom and checked all the stalls. Empty.

When he stepped into the men's room, one middle-aged man was at the sink, washing his hands.

"Did you see a woman come in here? Redhead?"

The man's eyes widened. "No. It's the men's room."

Ronin ducked out and strode down the hall. There was a side door leading outside. He pushed it open and looked around.

It opened to the museum parking lot. Except for parked cars, it was empty.

She was gone.

He frowned, stepping back inside. Who the hell was this mystery woman? And why had she crashed a wedding to watch them?

There was one thing that Ronin hated more than anything—mysteries. He always felt an overriding compulsion to solve them, especially when it came to protecting the few people in the world he cared about most.

***

Hale led Elin out onto the museum's rooftop deck. They leaned against the railing, looking out at the lights of Denver. A cool breeze brushed over them, and he wrapped his arms around her from behind, pulling her in close.

"Have I told you how good you look tonight?" he said.

"No." There was a smile in her voice.

He leaned down, pressing his lips to the side of her neck. "Well, Special Agent Alexander, you are going to get very lucky later."

She laughed, spinning in his arms. Then she went up on her toes and kissed him.

Just the taste of her was enough to have desire pulsing through him. Something told him it would always be like that with her, even when they were old and gray and surrounded by grandkids.

"Let's go home," she whispered.

Home. They could walk there from the museum. Hale had sold his one-bedroom bachelor pad, and together, they'd just purchased a two-bedroom condo only a few blocks away from City Park. It was theirs, and it was home.

"You're happy here?" he asked.

"I love Denver," she answered. "And I love you."

"The job in Europe—"

Her hands gripped his shirt and she shook him. "I'm happy. No regrets."

God, he'd gotten so lucky finding her. Hell, he was almost thankful to Silk Road. "I love you, too. I have something for you."

He led her over to a nearby chair and urged her to sit down. Then, he pulled a small box from his pocket and went down on one knee.

Her eyes went wide. "Hale..."

He held up the box.

She stared at it, then him, her mouth falling open.

"Have I made you speechless again?" he teased.

She didn't look like she was breathing. He wrapped her hand around the box and she gingerly opened it.

A tiny charm of the Eiffel Tower was nestled in the center.

The air rushed out of her and she smiled. "It's gorgeous. Thank you." She lifted the charm from the silk and then she gasped.

Hale felt a rush of nerves.

"Oh, my God, Hale," she breathed. "It's enormous."

The large diamond nestled on the platinum band sparkled in the light.

"It's the size of an ice-skating rink." She lifted her gaze to his.

"Marry me, Elin. I'm already yours, but I want

the world to know."

"How can you afford something like this?" She lifted the ring out.

"Well, you'll be the first woman in the world with an engagement ring that contains a diamond from King Solomon's Mines."

She froze. "You stole a diamond from Ophir?" Her voice turned high-pitched at the end.

"It just happened to be in my pocket when we got back. I thought it was pretty fitting." He lowered his voice. "Every time I look at it, I'll remember exactly where I was when I fell in love with the smartest, toughest, sexiest woman I've ever met."

Her face softened.

"And...ah, I *can* actually afford it," he told her.

Her brow wrinkled. "What?"

"I only found out today, and haven't had a chance to tell you...but thanks to Dec's contacts, it looks like I have a contract with the Navy to purchase my grappling gun design."

"What?" she said again.

"And there are millions involved." He still couldn't quite believe it.

"Oh, my God, Hale." She threw her arms around him. "Congratulations!"

"Thanks."

"So, looks like I'm going to marry a millionaire." She held her hand up.

Exhilaration burst through Hale. He took the ring and slid it onto her finger. Damn, it looked good there. He was much happier about the fact that Elin was his than any contract for millions of dollars.

"Do you want a big, splashy wedding, or something small and intimate?" He didn't care what they did, as long as she was by his side.

"As long as you're there, I don't mind." She leaned forward and pressed her lips to his. "How about we shoot for something in the middle?"

"Sounds perfect." He lifted up the Eiffel Tower charm. "And this is where we're going to have our honeymoon."

She grinned at him. "Sounds perfect to me."

I hope you enjoyed Elin and Hale's story! There are more Treasure Hunter Security adventures on the way! The series will continue with UNMAPPED, starring Ronin and his mystery woman coming in September 2017.

For more action-packed romance, read on for a preview of the first chapter of *Among Galactic Ruins,* the first book in my award-winning Phoenix Adventures series. This is action, adventure, romance and treasure hunting in space!

Don't miss out! For updates about new releases, action romance info, free books, and other fun stuff, sign up for my VIP mailing list and get your *free box set* containing three action-packed romances.

Visit here to get started:

www.annahackettbooks.com

FREE BOX SET DOWNLOAD

JOIN THE ACTION-PACKED ADVENTURE!

Formats: Kindle, ePub, PDF

Preview: Among Galactic Ruins

MORE ACTION ROMANCE?

**ACTION
ADVENTURE
TREASURE HUNTS
SEXY SCI-FI ROMANCE**

As the descending starship hit turbulence, Dr. Alexa Carter gasped, her stomach jumping.

But she didn't feel sick, she felt *exhilarated*.

She stared out the window at the sand dunes of the planet below. Zerzura. The legendary planet packed with danger, mystery and history.

She was *finally* here. All she could see was sand dune, after yellow sand dune, all the way off into the distance. The dual suns hung in the sky, big and full—one gold and one red—baking the ground below.

But there was more to Zerzura than that. She knew, from all her extensive history training as an astro-archeologist, that the planet was covered in ruins—some old and others beyond ancient. She knew every single one of the myths and legends.

She glanced down at her lap and clutched the Sync communicator she was holding. Right here she had her ticket to finding an ancient Terran treasure.

Lexa thumbed the screen. She'd found the slim, ancient vase in the museum archives and initially thought nothing of the lovely etchings of priestesses on the side of it.

Until she'd finished translating the obscure text.

She'd been gobsmacked when she realized the text gave her clues that not only formed a map, but also described what the treasure was at the end. A famed Fabergé egg.

Excitement zapped like electricity through her veins. After a career spent mostly in the Galactic Institute of Historical Preservation and on a few boring digs in the central systems, she was now the curator of the Darend Museum on Zeta Volantis—a private and well-funded museum that was mostly just a place for her wealthy patron, Marius Darend, to house his extensive, private collection of invaluable artifacts from around the galaxy.

But like most in the galaxy, he had a special obsession with old Earth artifacts. When she'd gone to him with the map and proposal to go on a treasure hunt to Zerzura to recover it, he'd been more than happy to fund it.

So here she was, Dr. Alexa Carter, on a treasure hunt.

Her father, of course, had almost had a coronary when she'd told her parents she'd be gone for several weeks. That familiar hard feeling invaded her belly. Baron Carter did not like his only daughter working, let alone being an astro-archeologist, and he *really* didn't like her going to a planet like Zerzura. He'd ranted about wild chases and wastes of time, and predicted her failure.

She straightened in her seat. She'd been ignoring her father's disapproval for years. When she had the egg in her hands, then he'd have to swallow his words.

Someone leaned over her, a broad shoulder brushing hers. "Strap in, Princess, we're about to land."

Lexa's excitement deflated a little. There was just one fly in her med gel.

Unfortunately, Marius had insisted she bring along the museum's new head of security. She didn't know much about Damon Malik, but she knew she didn't like him. The rumor among the museum staff was that he had a super-secret military background.

She looked at him now, all long, and lean and dark. He had hair as black as her own, but skin far darker. She couldn't see him in the military. His manner was too...well, she wasn't sure what, exactly, but he certainly didn't seem the type to happily take orders.

No, he preferred to be the one giving them.

He shot her a small smile, but it didn't reach his dark eyes. Those midnight-blue eyes were always...intense. Piercing. Like he was assessing everything, calculating. She found it unsettling.

"I'm already strapped in, Mr. Malik." She tugged on her harness and raised a brow.

"Just checking. I'm here to make sure you don't get hurt on this little escapade."

"Escapade?" She bit her tongue and counted to ten. "We have a map leading to the location of a very valuable artifact. That's hardly an escapade."

"Whatever helps you sleep at night, Princess." He shot a glance at the window and the unforgiving desert below. "This is a foolish risk for some silly egg."

She huffed out a breath. Infuriating man. "Why get a job at a museum if you think artifacts are silly?"

He leaned back in his seat. "Because I needed a change. One where no one tried to kill me."

Kill him? She narrowed her eyes and wondered again just what the hell he'd done before he'd arrived at the Darend.

A chime sounded and the pilot's voice filtered into the plush cabin of Marius' starship. "Landing at Kharga spaceport in three minutes. Hang on, ladies and gentlemen."

Excitement filled Lexa's belly. Ignoring the man beside her, she looked out the window again.

The town of Kharga was visible now. They flew directly over it, and she marveled at the primitive look and the rough architecture. The buildings were made of stone—some simple squares, others with domed roofs, and some a haphazard sprawl of both. In the dirt-lined streets, ragged beasts were led by robed locals, and battered desert speeders flew in every direction, hovering off the ground.

It wasn't advanced and yes, it was rough and dangerous. So very different to the marble-lined floors and grandeur of the Darend Museum or the Institute's huge, imposing museums and research centers. And it was the complete opposite of the luxury she'd grown up with in the central systems.

She barely resisted bouncing in her seat like a child. She couldn't *wait* to get down there. She wasn't stupid, she knew there were risks, but could hold her own and she knew when to ask for help.

The ship touched down, a cloud of dust puffing past the window. Lexa ripped her harness off, trying—and failing—to contain her excitement.

"Wait." Damon grabbed her arm and pulled her back from the opening door. "I'll go first."

As he moved forward, she pulled a face at his broad back. *Arrogant know-it-all.*

The door opened with a quiet hiss. She watched him stop at the top of the three steps that had extended from the starship. He scanned the spaceport...well, spaceport was a generous word for it. Lexa wasn't sure the sandy ground, beaten-up starships lined up beside them, and the battered buildings covered with black streaks—were those laser scorch marks?—warranted the term spaceport, but it was what it was.

Damon checked the laser pistols holstered at his lean hips then nodded. "All right." He headed down the steps.

Lexa tugged on the white shirt tucked into her fitted khaki pants. Mr. Dark and Brooding might be dressed in all black, but she'd finally pulled her rarely used expedition clothes out of her closet for the trip. She couldn't wait to get them dirty. She tucked her Sync into her small backpack, swung the bag over her shoulder and headed down the stairs.

"Our contact is supposed to meet us here." She looked around but didn't see anyone paying them much attention. A rough-looking freighter crew lounged near a starfreighter that didn't even look like it could make it off the ground. A couple of robed humanoids argued with three smaller-statured reptilians. "He's a local treasure hunter called Brocken Phoenix."

Damon grunted. "Looks like he's late. I suggest we head to the central market and ask around."

"Okay." She was eager to see more of Kharga and soak it all in.

"Stay close to me."

Did he have to use that autocratic tone all the time? She tossed him a salute.

Something moved through his dark eyes before he shook his head and started off down the dusty street.

As they neared the market, the crowds thickened. The noise increased as well. People had set up makeshift stalls, tables, and tents and were selling…well, just about everything.

There was a hawker calling out the features of his droids. Lexa raised a brow. The array available was interesting—from stocky maintenance droids to life-like syndroids made to look like humans.

Other sellers were offering clothes, food, weapons, collectibles, even dragon bones.

Then she saw the cages.

She gasped. "Slavers."

Damon looked over and his face hardened. "Yeah."

The first cage held men. All tall and well-built. Laborers. The second held women. Anger shot through her. "It can't be legal."

"We're a long way from the central systems, Princess. You'll find lots of stuff here on Zerzura that isn't legal."

"We have to—"

He raised a lazy brow. "Do something? Unless you've got a whole bunch of e-creds I don't know about or an army in your back pocket, there isn't much we can do."

Her stomach turned over and she looked away. He might be right, but did he have to be so cold about it?

"Look." He pointed deeper into the market at a dusty, domed building with a glowing neon sign above the door. "That bar is where I hear the treasure hunters gather."

She wondered how he'd heard anything about the place when they'd only been dirtside a few minutes. But she followed him toward the bar, casting one last glance at the slaves.

As they neared the building, a body flew outward through the arched doorway. The man hit the dirt, groaning. He tried to stand before flopping face first back into the sand.

Even from where they stood, Lexa smelled the liquor fumes wafting off him. Nothing smooth and sweet like what was available back on Zeta Volantis. No, this smelled like homebrewed rotgut.

Damon stepped over the man with barely a glance. At the bar entrance, he paused. "I think you should stay out here. It'll be safer. I'll find out what I can about Phoenix and be right back."

She wanted to argue, but right then, two huge giants slammed out of the bar, wrestling each other. One was an enormous man, almost seven feet tall, with some aquatic heritage. He had pale-blue skin, large, wide-set eyes and tiny gills on the side of his neck. His opponent was human with a mass of dreadlocked brown hair, who stood almost as tall and broad.

The human slammed a giant fist into the aquatic's face, shouting in a language Lexa's lingual implant didn't recognize. That's when Lexa realized the dreadlocked man was actually a woman.

A security droid floated out of the bar. Its laser weapons swiveled to aim at the fighting pair. "You are no longer welcome at the Desert Dragon. Please vacate the premises."

Grumbling, the fighters pulled apart, then shuffled off down the street.

Lexa swallowed. "Fine. I'll stay out here."

"Stay close," Damon warned.

She tossed him another mock salute and when he scowled, she felt a savage sense of satisfaction. Then he turned and ducked inside.

She turned back to study the street. One building down, she saw a stall holder standing behind a table covered in what looked like small artifacts. Lexa's heart thumped. She had to take a look.

"All original. Found here on Zerzura." The older man spread his arms out over his wares. "Very, very old." His eyes glowed in his ageless face topped by salt-and-pepper hair. "Very valuable."

"May I?" Lexa indicated a small, weathered statue.

The man nodded. "But you break, you buy."

Lexa studied the small figurine. It was supposed to resemble a Terran fertility statue—a woman with generous hips and breasts. She tested the weight of it before she sniffed and set it down. "It's not a very good fake. I'd say you create a wire mesh frame, set it in a mold, then pour a synthetic plas in. You finish it off by spraying it with some sort of rock texture."

The man's mouth slid into a frown.

Lexa studied the other items. Jewelry, small boxes and inscribed stones. She fingered a necklace. It was by no means old but it was pretty.

Then she spotted it.

A small, red egg, covered in gold-metalwork and resting on a little stand.

She picked it up, cradling its slight weight. The craftwork was terrible but there was no doubt it was a replica of a Fabergé egg.

"What is this?" she asked the man.

He shrugged. "Lots of myths about the Orphic

Priestesses around here. They lived over a thousand years ago and the egg was their symbol."

Lexa stroked the egg.

The man's keen eyes narrowed in on her. "It's a pretty piece. Said to be made in the image of the priestesses' most valuable treasure, the Goddess Egg. It was covered in Terran rubies and gold."

A basic history. Lexa knew from her research that the Goddess Egg had been brought to Zerzura by Terran colonists escaping the Terran war and had been made by a famed jeweler on Earth named Fabergé. Unfortunately, most of its history had been lost.

Someone bumped into Lexa from behind. She ignored it, shifting closer to the table.

Then a hard hand clamped down on her elbow and jerked her backward. The little red egg fell into the sand.

Lexa expected the cranky stall owner to squawk about the egg and demand payment. Instead, he scampered backward with wide eyes and turned away.

Lexa's accoster jerked her around.

"Hey," she exclaimed.

Then she looked up. Way up.

The man was part-reptilian, with iridescent scales covering his enormous frame. He stood somewhere over six and a half feet with a tough face that looked squashed.

"Let me go." She slapped at his hand. *Idiot.*

He was startled for a second and did release her. Then he scowled, which turned his face from frightening to terrifying. "Give me your e-creds." He grabbed her arm, large fingers biting into her flesh, and shook her. "I want everything transferred to my account."

Lexa raised a brow. "Or what?"

With his other hand, he withdrew a knife the length of her forearm. "Or I use this."

The Phoenix Adventures
Among Galactic Ruins
At Star's End
In the Devil's Nebula
On a Rogue Planet
Beneath a Trojan Moon
Beyond Galaxy's Edge
On a Cyborg Planet
Return to Dark Earth
On a Barbarian World
Lost in Barbarian Space
Through Uncharted Space

Also by Anna Hackett

Treasure Hunter Security
Undiscovered
Uncharted
Unexplored
Unfathomed

In the Devil's Nebula
On a Rogue Planet
Beneath a Trojan Moon
Beyond Galaxy's Edge
On a Cyborg Planet
Return to Dark Earth
On a Barbarian World
Lost in Barbarian Space
Through Uncharted Space

Perma Series
Winter Fusion

Warriors of the Wind
Tempest
Storm & Seduction
Fury & Darkness

Standalone Titles
Savage Dragon
Hunter's Surrender
One Night with the Wolf

Anthologies
A Galactic Holiday
Moonlight (UK only)
Vampire Hunter (UK only)
Awakening the Dragon (UK Only)

For more information visit AnnaHackettBooks.com

About the Author

I'm a USA Today bestselling author and I'm passionate about *action romance*. I love stories that combine the thrill of falling in love with the excitement of action, danger and adventure. I'm a sucker for that moment when the team is walking in slow motion, shoulder-to-shoulder heading off into battle.

I write about people overcoming unbeatable odds and achieving seemingly impossible goals. I like to believe it's possible for all of us to do the same.

My books are mixture of action, adventure and sexy romance and they're recommended for anyone who enjoys fast-paced stories where the boy wins the girl at the end (or sometimes the girl wins the boy!)

For release dates, action romance info, free books, and other fun stuff, sign up for the latest news here:

Website: AnnaHackettBooks.com

Made in United States
North Haven, CT
21 October 2023

43003558R10136